CRITICAL ACCLAIM FOR
K.C. CONSTANTINE AND
SUNSHINE ENEMIES

"Constantine knows his turf and its people as well as Tony Hillerman knows the Navaho-Hopi Southwest or Raymond Chandler knew southern California."

—*Los Angeles Times*

•

"Crime fiction has no shortage of strong central characters, but Balzic is special. Falstaffian in both his joys and his sufferings, he drinks, he swears, he swaggers . . . don't miss *Sunshine Enemies*."

—*Philadelphia Inquirer*

•

"Even more than Wambaugh, K.C. Constantine has been nudging the police procedural into literature . . . nobody writes better dialogue."

—*Detroit News*

•

"Over the years, the Balzic novels have moved beyond the conventions of the police procedural genre. They now constitute a sustained series of American regional fiction with marvelous evocations of character, place and time."

—*Washington Post Book World*

•

"In *Sunshine Enemies*, K.C. Constantine shows what a serious crime writer can accomplish . . . a novel that ticks with life."

—*Newsweek*

•

"Nobody, but nobody, has K.C. Constantine's ear for the working-class dialect of Middle America."

—*Boston Herald*

•

"You won't find the town of Rocksburg, Pa., on any map; but to fans of K.C. Constantine's realer-than-real police procedurals, the two-bit, working-class burg has all the feel of home . . . Mr. Constantine's compassionate blue-collar cop speaks with unusual eloquence here."

—*New York Times Book Review*

K.C. Constantine's
Mario Balzic Novels

Sunshine Enemies
Joey's Case
Upon Some Midnights Clear
Always a Body to Trade
The Man Who Liked Slow Tomatoes
A Fix Like This
The Blank Page
The Man Who Liked to Look at Himself
The Rocksburg Railroad Murders

K·C·CONSTANTINE
SUNSHINE ENEMIES

THE MYSTERIOUS PRESS

New York • Tokyo • Sweden • Milan

Published by Warner Books

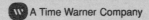 A Time Warner Company

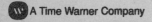

The man with the clerical collar tottered bowlegged under the weight of his cargo into Balzic's office. Flushed, sweaty, breathing loudly, he dumped a pile of magazines a foot and a half high on Balzic's desk, groaned in relief, leaned back from the waist, and seemed to be trying to realign his spine with his thumbs. After a few seconds of this self-chiropractic, he groaned again, fumbled for a handkerchief in the pocket of his pearl-gray suitcoat, found it, and wiped his brow, face, and neck, his breathing only slightly less noisy than when he'd first come through the door.

"Something I can do for you?" Balzic said, leaning back in his chair, drumming his thumbs on the armrests.

"P. Shaner Weier," the cleric said, holding out his soft, damp hand almost at shoulder level, forcing Balzic to stand to shake it. "And there certainly is something you can do for me. And for yourself. And for this city. You can dig a deep hole and bury this." He pointed, not only with his index finger, but with his gaze, his nose, his shoulders, his protuberant belly, at the pile of magazines he'd just dropped onto Balzic's desk. "This excrement, this poison is polluting our city, our children, our lives,

1

our souls. And I don't think you know about this. And the reason I don't think you know about this is because if you did you'd be out there with a can of gasoline and a match or a bulldozer or something to destroy this—this unspeakable filth."

Balzic rubbed his forehead. "You're talkin' about the porn store that just opened up out on the, uh—"

"Out on the fringe of our city, on the edge of our community, on the far reaches of our civic soul. Yes. That store is my aim. Our aim. Yours and mine. Our enemy. It is a land filled with unsanitary things. It is a dump."

"Well, you're probably right," Balzic said, "but I'd really rather not get into it."

"I beg your pardon?"

"Uh, I see you've got a turned-around collar, but I don't know you. Where exactly are you the reverend of?"

"The Lutheran church."

"In Rocksburg?"

"Of course in Rocksburg."

"I didn't even know there was one."

"We're small, no doubt of that. Barely fifty members. But we're here. We're vigorous. We're committed."

"And how long have *you* been here, exactly?"

"I answered my call a week ago."

"That means you've been here a week?"

"Yes, of course. Isn't that what I just said?"

"Well, I probably misunderstood—"

"How long *I've* been here is quite beside the point," Weier said, "which point is, this despicable by-product of the lewd and lascivious minds of despicable, uh, uh, I loathe to call them people. But, of course, they are. We can hardly blame this on giraffes or elephants or cows or dogs. This is the warped thinking of warped human minds."

Weier spun the magazine on top of the stack around and opened it. "Look at this! Just look at it!"

Balzic held up his hands. "I don't want to look at that stuff."

"Why not? How can you know your enemy if you refuse to confront him?"

"I've seen enough of that stuff to know what it is, I don't have to look at any more."

2

"Oh no. No! You have to look at this," Weier said, jabbing at the open magazine with his index finger. "This is one hundred percent pure unmitigated filth. There is absolutely no serious literary, artistic, political, educational, or scientific value here. This is patently offensive.

"This is stuff the average person, applying contemporary community standards, would find appeals to the prurient interest and to the prurient interest alone. This—"

"Uh, hold it, hold it, okay? I'm sure you're right about all of this, but I'm also sure of something else. This stuff, these magazines, this is a legal swamp, and I don't want any part of it."

"I beg your pardon?" Weier looked as though he'd just closed his mouth around spoiled food.

"Yeah, that's stuff I'm sure I wouldn't want my daughters to see and I sure as hell wouldn't want my mother to see and I'd probably get real nervous if my wife was standin' here, but that doesn't matter. That stuff's a legal minefield and I'm not gonna start tryin' to tippy-toe through it."

Weier now looked as though he'd spit out most of the spoiled food but couldn't get rid of the idea that he might have swallowed some. "Do I understand you? You are not going to do anything about this?" He pointed at the pile of magazines, his index finger quivering.

Balzic nodded several times slowly. He sighed, his chest falling heavily.

Weier began to sputter. "Because why? Be-be-because of the legal complications? The technicalities? Is that why?"

"You got it. That's exactly why."

"I do not believe—but you are the police, are you not?"

"I'm the chief here, yes."

"And you refuse to carry out your duty?"

"Well if you wanna put it in those words, yeah."

"But—but—but this is preposterous. You've taken an oath. You've sworn to uphold the law, not only of our federal government but of the state as well. And the state law is very clear about this sort of thing—"

"Whoa whoa whoa, it is not as clear as you're tryin' to make it—"

"Is this filth or not? Look at it. You still won't look at it. How can you see what you won't look at?"

"Look, Reverend Maier—"

"Weier. W-E-I-E-R."

"Sorry. Weier. Look. This stuff is whatever you want to call it—"

"No no no no no. It is absolutely *not* whatever I choose to call it. It is what any average person, applying contemporary community standards, would find appeals to the prurient interest and to the prurient interest alone—"

"You said that before."

"Because I was quoting the *Crimes Code* of this commonwealth."

"I know."

"Well, Chief—what is your name again?"

"Balzic. B-A-L-Z-I-C."

"Balzic. Is that Serbian? You look more Italian than Slavic."

"Half and half."

"Oh. Well. Where were we?"

"You were quoting the *Crimes Code*."

"Yes yes yes I was. Because that is what applies here. It is not a matter of personal taste or whimsy. What the state very wisely says is that 'any average person, applying contemporary community standards—'"

Balzic shook his head no and held up his hands. "See, right there, that's where you stepped on two mines: 'average person' and 'contemporary community standards.' Boom, boom. Both your legs gone, legally. 'Cause you get in the witness chair and start talkin' those two things, even a dumb lawyer'll eat you alive."

"I'd like to see him try."

Balzic snorted. "Okay. Go find me an average person and bring him back here. And make sure he can recite, without any help from you or anybody else, all the community standards we have here in Rocksburg."

"Oh well, but you're being facetious."

"I'm what?"

"Facetious. Funny. You're making a joke."

"No I'm not."

"Well then you don't understand statistical probabilities that translate into community beliefs."

Balzic sighed and swore under his breath. He looked over his glasses at the Reverend Weier, who was now perspiring freely, though the room was on the cool side, nearer to sixty-eight degrees than to seventy.

"Uh, Reverend, do you think that you and a Catholic priest would have a lot more in common, statistically speaking, than, say, you and a pimp?"

"Why of course."

"So then we could talk about community standards a lot easier with you and the priest, right? Than with you and the pimp, right?"

"I would certainly hope so."

"Okay, so then tell me what the community standards are about priests and reverends being married, you wanna do that?"

"What you're doing, Chief Balzer—"

"Balzic."

"Balzic. Yes. What you're doing is setting up hypothetical situations to knock them down to make your arguments look invincible. It's an old trick in debate. I know. I was a debater for many years."

"Well I wasn't a debater, but what I'm trying to tell you is that between two people—you and a Catholic priest—two people who should have a lot in common, there's a whole lot of room for argument, that's what I'm sayin'. For instance, you wanna tell me the community standard around here for the infallibility of the pope, huh? The pope's always right, right?"

"Well of course there will be differences there, but both of us—me and this hypothetical priest of yours—we have much more to agree about than the life of Christ."

"So if you two have so much in common, you both have this solid set of standards to go on, how come you're the first preacher, priest, rabbi, whatever, to come in here with a beef about the porn store?"

"You can't be serious. No one else from the ministerium?"

"From the what?"

5

"The ministerium, the association of clerics—priests, preachers?"

"Uh, no. Nobody. Just you."

"Well." Weier heaved a large sigh. "I see I've got some work cut out for me."

"Looks that way. Uh, Reverend, where'd you come from? D'you have a church somewhere else?"

"Lawrence County. New Castle. Why do you ask?"

"Just curious," Balzic said, shrugging.

"Well, I suppose I need to go talk to the ministerium," Weier said, nodding ponderously many times and backing out of Balzic's office with a feeble wave. His shirtfront was clotted with sweat.

"Uh, hold it, Reverend. Hold it."

Weier came forward hesitantly. "Yes?"

"Uh, take this stuff with you, okay? I don't want this stuff layin' around here."

"Oh. Yes. Of course." Weier came forward, swept the magazines into his arms, and wobbled out, his legs bowing under their weight.

Balzic waited for a minute, then he went out to the radio console and found Desk Sergeant Vic Stramsky working a crossword puzzle.

"Hey, Vic, try to find Rugs Carlucci, will ya? Tell him to call me."

Stramsky nodded, stifled a yawn, and started making calls. Balzic went back to his office and had just sat down when his phone rang. It was Carlucci.

"Hey, Rugs, when you get a chance, run down a guy claims to be a Lutheran minister. P. Shaner Weier." Balzic spelled it.

"Whatta you lookin' for, Mario?"

"This guy just landed in town about a week ago, says he used to have a church in New Castle, Lawrence County. I don't know what's with the guy—maybe he sweats too hard, I don't know. Just see if he's who he says he is. No hurry."

"Okay, Mario. Give me a couple of days, I'm workin' a couple of things, and I'm gonna be in court all day for the next two days."

"Okay. Whenever. See ya."

Balzic picked up the phone book and looked for the Lutheran listing under churches in the Yellow Pages. There was one listed, but it wasn't in Rocksburg. It was in Westfield Township, which abutted Rocksburg on two sides. Balzic then opened the *City Directory* and found no listing for a Lutheran church in the city.

He pushed that book aside, found the number for the Lutheran church in Westfield Township in the phone book, and punched the buttons for the rectory.

A woman answered. Balzic identified himself and asked who the woman was.

"My husband is the minister of this congregation."

"And your name, ma'am?"

"Shanefelt. Mrs. Roger Shanefelt. My name is Lucinda."

"I see. Uh, does the name Weier mean anything to you, ma'am?"

"No," she said after a moment. "I don't recognize the name. Should I?"

"I don't know, ma'am. Does your husband have an assistant?"

"No."

"Is he supposed to get an assistant in the near future?"

"Not that I know of."

"Could this be the sort of thing you would not normally know about?"

"I don't know what you're getting at, but *I* am my husband's assistant. I don't assist him with his clerical duties, of course, but I most certainly do help him with every other phase of his ministry and I most certainly would know if he *was* getting an assistant. I do know that he's never requested one; our congregation isn't nearly large enough to justify such a position, and we've never even discussed it. It's never come into our conversations. Why are you asking these questions?"

"Oh it's just a routine check, ma'am. It's nothing really."

"Well who is this Meyer person?"

"Not Meyer. Weier. I just thought maybe you or your husband would know him, ma'am, that's all. Thank you very much for your help. Good-bye." Balzic hung up before she could ask any more questions.

He went back out to the duty room and stood in front of Stramsky, who was engrossed in his crossword puzzle.

Stramsky looked up. "Hey, Mario, what's a five-letter word for—?"

"Don't ask me about those things. How many times have I told you—those things are the work of cons, gettin' back at guys like you."

"Who told you that?"

"You always ask me that, who told me that? And I always tell you, 'I read it someplace.' I don't know where, but it figures. Who could take that kind of revenge better than cons? Who's got more time to figure those things out than some guy doin' four consecutive life terms? How else you gonna get even with society better than fuckin' with their minds makin' up crossword puzzles nobody can do?"

"Mario, don't take this wrong, but I think you made this theory of yours up 'cause you don't like to do crosswords. And I think you don't like to see me doin' 'em and you don't know how to tell me, so you tell me they're how the cons get back at me—at people like me. That's what I think."

Balzic scratched the underside of his chin with his thumbnail. He nodded several times. "You're right; I don't like to see you doin' 'em. I think it's the surest sign of a guy fuckin' off that I ever saw. I don't think it builds your vocabulary or develops your concentration or any of that shit people say doin' 'em does."

"The only people who say things like that are teachers."

"I heard lots of other people say that."

"Mario, it's just a puzzle, that's all it is. It ain't nothin' bigger than that."

"It doesn't look right when people walk in and see you doin' it."

"Mario, I put it down as soon as somebody opens the door. Nobody ever saw—no civilian ever saw me doin' one of these when I was supposed to be workin'. Honest."

Balzic turned away and stared off for a moment. "The goddamn things are stupid, Vic. You're supposed to come up with the names of things nobody ever uses."

Stramsky shrugged. "That's part of the fun, Mario."

8

Balzic sighed disgustedly. "How the hell can it be fun to find the answer for something that has nothin' to do with everyday reality?"

Stramsky shrugged again. "It's part of my everyday reality. I do two, three of these every day."

"Oh yeah? You know a lotta words from all these crosswords? Huh? Then what's the word for the Lutheran thing, uh, it's like the diocese?"

"Oh, that's the synod. Yeah. Five letters."

"What?"

"Synod. S-Y-N-O-D."

"So if I looked them up in the Pittsburgh phone book, that would be like callin' the diocese here?"

"Yeah. Right. Sure it would—I think."

Balzic started to walk away, then turned back. "Hey, Vic, you ever wanna play music?"

"Huh?"

"Music, you know. You ever wanna play it?"

"Uh, no. Why?"

"I don't know. I was in the mall the other day—Ruth was lookin' for a book, about some lady who's a beekeeper or somethin'—and I'm standin' there and I'm lookin' at all these shelves of stuff, they're not like books really—I mean they are but they aren't if you know what I mean—and my eyes keep comin' back to this book, *Harmonica for the Musical Idiot* or somethin' like that, and I keep hearin' this harmonica goin' through my head, some song I don't even know the name of. And I wanted to buy this damn book. You get a book and a harmonica and one of those cassette tapes, you know, ninety minutes long, and I'm standin' there lookin' at it and I keep hearin' this song and I'm lookin' at it, and this clerk comes up and says can she help me, and I put the book down like I just got caught shopliftin' and said, nah, no, I don't need any help.

"So Ruth comes and gets me—she got her book—and we leave, and all the way to the car I'm thinkin' I shoulda bought that damn book. . . . You never wanted to make music, huh?"

Stramsky shook his head no. "I whistle sometimes, but it ain't anythin' anybody could recognize, you know? And I could never sing worth shit. We had to try out for the chorus when I

9

started the ninth grade? I remember this teacher, real nice lady—what the hell was her name? Never mind. Anyway, she tried to get me to sing, I sounded like a fuckin' frog havin' a heart attack. I'll never forget the look on her face. She was real nice, you know, you could just see how much it hurt her just to listen to me. She patted me on the head, she said maybe I'd be better off if I went to woodshop instead of chorus. That was the nicest thing anybody said to me that whole year."

"Yeah, that's me too, pretty much," Balzic said dreamily. "But there was somethin' about this book I keep thinkin' about, I don't know what the hell it is. Maybe it's cause I always felt like a musical idiot, I don't know."

"Hey, sounds to me like you oughta buy the book."

"Nah. You kiddin'? You're supposed to learn how to play music when you're young, a little kid, kids learn faster—everybody knows that."

Stramsky shook his head no. "Who told you that? You remember Eddie Polansky? Worked in the post office? Retired a couple years ago?"

Balzic shrugged. "Vaguely."

"He was goin' nuts. His old lady practically ran his ass outta the house every day. He was walkin' the streets, nothin' to do. All he ever did his whole life was sort mail and watch TV, play cards, Bingo, and go bowlin'. But now he got forty hours empty every week."

"So he bought a violin and he's gonna play in a symphony, I guess."

"Nah nah, c'mon, listen to me here. There's a message here."

"So what is it?"

"Well lemme tell it. Quit interruptin' me."

"Tell the story, will ya? I'm not interruptin' you."

"So anyway, he's wanderin' around and he walks past the music store, up on Main Street? DeBone's place?"

"DeBone don't own that anymore. He's dead for crissake. His wife sold it five, six years ago. Band teacher in the junior high school bought it. I can't think of his name."

"Whoever. That's beside the point who owns it. Eddie walks in 'cause he never been inside before. He walked past that store every day on his way to the post office and on his way home every night for years and years and he was never in it. So he goes inside. Couple hours later he comes out with a balalaika."

"A what?"

"It's like a guitar or a banjo. Only it only got three strings. So, make a long story short, he's in one of those—uh, whatta you call 'em, tamburitzens—you know, singers and dancers and they play all kinds of Slavic music? He goes all over the goddamn place. Sold his car, bought a van, just got back from Michigan, last week he was in New York, he's on the road two days a week. He told me it was the greatest thing he ever did in his life was walkin' into that music store. He told me he was gettin' ready to take the bridge. Yeah. Ready to do the dive. And he's older than you are. So there's the moral of the story: Go buy the goddamn harmonica."

"I don't have forty hours a week I don't know what to do with."

Stramsky shrugged.

Before either of them could say anything else, the phone rang. Stramsky answered and, after a few seconds, punched a button and pointed to Balzic. "It's your wife," Stramsky said.

Balzic picked up a phone at another desk. "Yeah, Ruth, what's up?"

"Mario, it's your mother. I just called 911 for an ambulance and I just called Dr. James."

"What happened?"

"She just screwed up her face and she said, 'Oh God,' or something and then she fell back in her chair and when I asked her what was wrong, she just looked at me real funny and then her eyes closed and she shook her head real hard—I have to go. The ambulance is here. Meet me at the hospital."

"Oh shit," Balzic said, hanging up. "Somethin's wrong with my mother, Vic. I'm goin' to the hospital."

Balzic bolted out of the duty room, down the three concrete steps into the parking lot, and into his cruiser. He got to the emergency room of Conemaugh General Hospital before the ambulance did. By the time he'd found a parking space in the visitors' lot across the street, the ambulance was backing up to the doors at the main entrance to the trauma unit. He rushed across the street as the attendants were piling out and hustling around to the back.

Before Balzic could reach them, they had the rear doors of the ambulance open and the gurney on the concrete and rolling. His mother looked very small. Ruth was darting ahead, holding doors. Balzic caught up to her inside the waiting room as the gurney was disappearing into the treatment rooms.

Ruth held out her arms and walked into his chest. She sobbed, just once, then pulled her head back and looked at him.

"Jesus," he said, "I hope this isn't as serious as you look."

"Me too. But I think it is. I think she had a stroke, Mario. Just the way she acted, the way her face got all contorted, and the way she tried to shake her head—and then she just quit focusing."

"Okay okay, take it easy. Don't tell me any more. Let's go take care of the paper bullshit here, and then, uh, we'll just wait and see, okay?"

"Okay."

"Okay, so let's do that."

Balzic kissed her on the cheek and then on the lips, and they went to the admissions window.

"May I help you?" said the clerk, a thick woman with many rings on her fingers. Her hair was dyed auburn and was stiff with hairspray, and she kept tapping at the curls above her right temple. She did not look at either of them as she spoke.

"Uh, my mother was just brought in by Mutual Aid ambulance and her doctor's on his way now, so whatever information you want, just ask."

The clerk settled herself at the keyboard of a computer. "Last name?"

"Balzic."

"Is that her married name?"

"Yes."

She hit some keys and waited. "First name and maiden name?"

"Marie Petraglia."

She spelled all three names, typed some more, and waited. "She's been a patient here before, is that correct?"

"Yes. Several times."

"Here it is. Marie Petraglia Balzic. Okay. You just have a seat and I'll call you when I want you to sign the admitting sheet."

"You don't want to see any insurance cards?"

"Oh no. Her Medicare and Medicaid numbers are right here. I don't need to see anything. Just have a seat and I'll call you to sign the sheet as soon as it gets printed out. I said that, didn't I?"

"Yeah."

"Well if I said it twice, it must be right. Just have a seat."

Balzic led Ruth away to some molded plastic chairs, and they slumped into them.

"She tried to shake her head real hard, like an insect was getting in her eye and she waved her hand over . . ."

"That's okay, you don't have to tell me about it—unless you want to."

Ruth shrugged and shook her head. "I'm just talking. I'm not trying to say anything."

Moments later, the clerk called Balzic back to sign the admission form. After he did so, he went back and stood by Ruth for a second; then he turned abruptly and started toward the doors leading to the treatment rooms. He stopped, shook his head, and went back and sat beside Ruth.

"I was gonna go in there and see what I could do to help. I don't know what the hell I thought I was gonna do—direct traffic, I guess. . . . Jesus, I'm still a baby, you know it? That's my momma in there. . . . Right now I'm as scared as I've ever been. I wasn't this scared on Iwo Jima. And I was wearin' everything I had in me when I landed. Bowel, bladder, belly, it was all over me. And right now I feel like I'm gettin' ready to lose it all again."

"Why don't you go to the john?"

"Aw I won't lose it. I just feel all cold and tingly."

Balzic's right knee began to bounce up and down. "I wonder if James got here yet. Whatta you think?"

"We won't know until he's examined her anyway."

"I'd feel a whole helluva lot better if he was here. She always trusted him. She did, didn't she?"

"Sure. She thought he's—she thinks he's wonderful."

"You called him, right?"

Ruth patted his hand. "He'll be here. He will."

"He always made me nervous, you know that?"

"I know."

"Never made her nervous. She loves him. Thinks he's the greatest thing since pasta."

"I know."

"I know you know, I'm just talkin'." Balzic sighed, pushed his glasses up his nose, and felt them slide back down. He took his glasses off, took out a hanky, wiped his face, and put his glasses back on. In seconds, they were sliding again. "God am I sweatin'."

"Yesterday, we were on the deck, she was in the folding chair and I was on the cushion on my back and I was reading *A Country Year*—that book I bought?—and I read some parts to her. I told her a little bit about this woman—how she was starting over pretty late in life and trying to make a living selling honey—and she listened and then she said, 'Yeah, that's right,' or 'Yeah, that's how it was,' and I asked her if she knew anything about bees and she laughed real hard. She said, 'No no, I don't know nothing about bees. But all the rest, all that work on your own, starting all over by yourself, that's all true.' She was laughing. She wasn't the least resentful about that. And God, you know it had to be hard when she was trying to do it."

"Yeah, the only time I ever heard her bitch was when she told me the Jew doctors paid her more to clean their houses than the nuns paid her to clean their house. I don't think she ever got over that. I shouldn't say she was bitchin' about that, 'cause she wasn't. She was more, uh, bewildered, confused, you know, like 'How can this be?' 'Cause the nuns, you know, they think you're supposed to want to work for nothin'. They take a vow of poverty, they think everybody's supposed to take a vow of poverty, and if you don't, you know—what the hell am I tellin' you for? You know how they are. But Ma, you know, she never put 'em down. She'd just go everywhere before she'd go to the nuns. And the first time somebody would offer her somethin', pishewwww! Gone. Off and runnin'. Do anything but work for the goddamn nuns. And if she heard me now, she'd try to give me a smack."

Balzic's eyes glazed over for a long moment. "I'm gonna tell you when Ma turned into King Kong. I never told you this.

"I was in the ninth grade and I knew she couldn't afford to send me to Central Catholic. I knew she couldn't. I knew I was a hardship case, but I knew she had to pay something. I didn't know what it was. But the point is, I knew she owed the nuns, you know, for gettin' me in.

"So one day this little nun showed up—she was about four feet six. And her face was all twisted up. This was a woman who had never smiled in her life—if she'd've smiled she'd've got charley horses in her cheeks. She was out at the home for the real real retarded and handicapped kids, and I guess they couldn't put up with her so they transferred her to Central. So I'm walkin' down the hall to the principal's office with the absentee list this one day and she comes out of nowhere and wants to know what I think I'm doin'. And I told her, I was goin' to the principal's office and bang! I'm up against the wall, my head's full of mosquitoes and I look down at my shirt, there's blood all over it. She hit me with the hard side of a blackboard eraser right across the ear and my ear just split and Kee-rist there was blood everywhere, mostly on my white shirt.

"I got so scared I ran out of the building and all the way home. 'Cause I was scared what Ma was gonna do when she saw the shirt—you know, the shirt was ruined. And it never occurred to me that the nun was wrong. A nun's a nun, right? Well it was one of those goofy coincidences, Ma got to work that day, wherever it was, and they told her they didn't need her, so she went home. And I guess she was really pissed off about that, and then here I came, and she saw me and when she got it outta me what happened, she grabbed my hand and just pulled me along right back to school—I mean, after she cleaned me off and chipped off some ice and made me hold it on my ear. She went straight for the principal's office. She never said a word. I was so scared, I didn't know what was gonna happen. She went inside old Sister Mary Joseph's office, she said she wanted to talk to the nun that hit me. So we spent about five minutes of me tryin' to tell what happened and what the nun looked like and all that, and I still had the absentee list in my pocket, so I gave it to Sister Mary Joseph. And then off she goes and she comes back about five minutes later with the nun that belted me. And my whole body was shakin'.

"And Ma says, 'Did you hit my son?' And she says yeah, sure. And Ma asks her to look at my shirt—would she agree the shirt was ruined? And I forget what the nun said. And then Ma asked her why she didn't try to stop me, to help me, couldn't she see I was cut? I was bleedin'? And the nun said, 'God wanted him to bleed so he'd learn to honor his elders.' And Ma asked her if she'd asked me what I was doin' in the hall. And she said no, why should she ask me that, nobody was supposed to be in the hall then, and I'll never forget what happened then—man oh man, she hauled off and kicked that nun right in the shin. I mean, that nun screamed, and tried to hold her ankle, she was hoppin' up and down on one foot, and then she lost her balance and fell over.

"Ma just looked at her, then she shook her finger at her and she said, 'Don't you ever do that again.' Then she grabbed me and walked me up to the hospital and they put a couple stitches in my ear. And the people there wanted her to pay for it and they started to hassle her and she told 'em, 'Send the bill to Central Catholic High School—a nun hit him, the nuns are gonna pay for it.' And that was the end of that.

"And, man, from that day on, I knew nobody could ever hurt me, not as long as my momma was there, 'cause by god she'd get 'em. And I was terrified of her. I was terrified of ever doin' anything that would make her be embarrassed or ashamed. I was scared to death of not makin' her proud of me. I knew if I ever did anything to humiliate her, I mean, you talk about callin' for backup. Jesus. And I knew tonight, when I saw her on the gurney, it was all over. I never saw her look so small. . . . Jesus Christ, Ruth, I'm gonna be on my own out there. . . ."

Ruth took his right hand in both her hands and lifted it to her lips and kissed it. "I know," she said. "I know."

A long moment passed, then Ruth said, "Mario, I, uh, you've told me that story before."

"Huh? I have?"

"The first time was right before I was going to meet her."

"Really? I told you then?"

Ruth nodded.

"Geez, I never thought—I thought I never told you that before."

"Many times, Mario."

"Many times? Really?"

"Many times. Really."

"Well, uh, you know, why didn't you say so?"

Ruth sighed. "The first time, she never touched the nun. She just shook her finger in her face."

"Huh. Really? So, uh, I didn't tell it always the same? So when'd I start changin' it?"

"I can't remember for sure. I think it was about ten years ago she started punching her, knockin' her out. One time she broke her nose, another time she split her lip. They were all one-punch knockouts though."

Balzic sighed. "Uh, did I—d'you ever tell me I told you before?"

"Every time. No, not the second time. I didn't tell you till the third time. But I told you every time since. And I have to tell you now, this kick in the shins, this is new."

"Aw, Ruth, you're such a pain in the ass sometimes. Your memory's too good."

Ruth nodded. "It's one of my jobs. Just like cleanin' the bathroom. I think it's a state law, you have to clean the bathroom, you have to remember all the stories."

Balzic tried to smile at her, but his eyes filled up. He turned away.

"Mario, she told me what happened. It's a lot worse, a lot scarier than you remember. She didn't touch the nun, she just told her that if she ever touched you again without a good reason, she'd put the *mal occhio* on her, the evil eye. The nun fell down all right. She fainted. But it wasn't the little nun, the one who smacked you. It was Sister Mary Joseph, the principal."

Balzic turned back to her, his eyes wide. "Honest to God, is that what happened?"

"Honest to God, that's what happened. That's why you think your mother's so powerful. She knocked the principal out without touchin' her."

"Jesus Christ," Balzic said. "You're right. That's what happened. Jesus. Imagine. Did I ever tell it right?"

17

"Nope. Not once."

"No wonder I was terrified of her."

"You never talked about it with her, did you?"

"You kiddin'? Hell, no, I never talked about it. Christ, that was real power there. Put a nun on her back without ever touchin' her? You think I'm gonna discuss that with the person who did it? I never knew until this minute how I tried to dance around it. Look how long I've been dancin' around it. How old are you in the ninth grade? Fourteen?" Balzic stared off into space and shook his head.

They fell silent. He slipped his hand into hers, and they sat that way for many minutes. Eventually, they started flipping through old magazines and showing each other articles and cartoons, but they both knew they were just doing it to pass the time and so they had to work just to smile.

Balzic found himself in that crazy time limbo where he was looking at his watch every few minutes and yet couldn't say with any certainty how long he'd been looking at his watch.

People came and went, some with wracking coughs, others with halting, ungainly steps, others with bloody cloths wrapped around fingers. One man came in with a tooth in a plastic sandwich bag and started soliciting opinions from everybody in the waiting room whether it could be replaced in his mouth. He was seventy years old, he said, and he only had eleven teeth left, and his girlfriend had to go and knock out one of those. She was seventy-one, he said, and she hadn't had her own teeth since she was forty and so she didn't understand how important one tooth could be.

About then, Dr. Bradford James came out and found them and led them down the hall so they could have some privacy.

After some awkward amenities, he said, "I wish I had better news, but I'm afraid she's had a major cardiovascular accident. I won't know to what extent until we've run some tests, but it's obvious she can't use her right hand and arm, and she can't speak, and the muscle tone on the right side of her face is diminished."

"She's had a stroke then?" Balzic said.

"That's as good a word as any other, at this point."

"What's it look like?"

18

James sighed and shrugged. "What I'm most concerned about is renal failure. Her kidneys have been deteriorating for several years now, and, while I won't know until I see the test results, I am concerned that she may lose the kidney on the right side. It's almost automatic in a CVA of this magnitude. Or I should say, of this apparent magnitude. I don't want to alarm you unnecessarily, but, well, I'd be telling less than the truth if I told you anything other than that it doesn't look real good. How old is she?"

"Eighty," Balzic said.

"Eighty-one," Ruth said.

James shrugged. "She's had a good life."

"Well it's not finished yet," Balzic said sharply.

"I didn't say that," James said. "I just meant that, uh, your mother is a special person. I like to think that we were friends. I never BS'd her and she never BS'd me. I think that if she'd been unhappy with her life, she would have told me. She never did. She wasn't any Pollyanna. She was a direct woman, always to the point. She was also very funny. Not that she came in telling jokes—she didn't. But she has a sense of humor based on an, a really unadorned sense of reality. Why am I defending myself?"

"'Cause you started talking in the past tense," Ruth said. She was smiling and congenial, but no less serious because of that.

James straightened his shoulders and then let them drop with a long sigh. "The hardest thing to say sometimes is what's most obvious, and that's because we don't always want to look at what's most obvious. What's obvious here is that Marie is eighty-one, she has a history of renal dysfunction, and she has suffered what appears to be a major CVA. None of which detracts from the fact or diminishes the fact that she has had a good life, and that I have long thought of her as a friend and that I hope she thinks of me that way. Also—and this is very important—no matter what I said about her life a moment ago, I am not going to do anything less than my best to care for her now."

"Uh, Doc, you don't have to say anymore."

James licked his upper lip. "I didn't have to say that much,

19

quite frankly, but I didn't want there to be any misunderstanding."

James excused himself, and Balzic and Ruth went back to the waiting room. A young mother had brought her infant daughter in, and for nearly half an hour the two tried to make the young mother feel comfortable. She wasn't married, she had no insurance; all she knew was her baby wasn't feeling good.

Ruth kept asking what was wrong with the baby—it looked just fine to her.

After nearly twenty-five minutes of this sort of conversation, the girl said, "My dad . . . my dad took me to the front door and pushed me out on the porch, and he said I was a tramp and a whore and he wouldn't have me living in his house anymore. Then he just shut the door. . . . And I went around the back and I knocked and knocked and my mom would not open the door. . . . I could understand my dad doin' that. It's just been killin' him ever since I started to show . . . but I never thought my mom would just let me go like that . . . I mean, they didn't even let me get any diapers. . . ." She just shook her head and shrugged. She looked at her baby the whole time she spoke; she never once looked at Ruth or Balzic.

Ruth's hand went to her mouth. "My god. Mario, did you hear?"

Balzic nodded. "Uh, young lady, does the father of this baby know he's a father?"

She shook her head no.

"So your father's stuck with not only you, but he's also stuck with his granddaughter."

"Mario! For god's sake."

"Hey, I'm just tellin' you everybody's got a point of view, you know?"

"Well I don't think she has to hear that. Not now."

"Nobody has to hear anything, ever. That's why all the old people are watchin' TV and all the kids are listenin' to their tape players. Every once in a while somebody gotta turn the artificial reality off and get a little of the real stuff. And, naturally, that pisses people off and makes 'em mad at the guys pushin' reality. Me, in other words. So, uh, what's your name, young lady, and what's your phone number?"

"Why? What are you going to do? Who are you?"

"I'm chief of police here." Balzic produced his ID case and held it out so the mother could compare the picture with the face.

"What are you going to do?"

"I'm gonna call your father is what I'm gonna do."

"Oh you can't do that. You don't know my father. He's . . . you don't argue with my father. He's never wrong. Never. He talks to God. And God talks to him. And he just knows."

"Well, you let me talk to him, I'll see what I can do."

"Well you're just going—all you're going to do is, you'll just make him madder. And if you make him madder—I mean, madder than he is—he'll never let me come home."

"So how long you think it'll be before he cools off enough for you to come home? Couple days? A week?"

"Oh no. Longer than that. Way longer than that."

"Where you think you're gonna live in the meantime?"

She shrugged. "I sort of thought, you know, here."

"You mean here? The waiting room? Is this the 'here' you mean?"

"Yeah, well, you know, they wouldn't let us starve."

Balzic closed his eyes and exhaled loudly through his nose. "Little girl, little girl, this is a hospital. It's run nonprofit, they're not out to make money, but they don't do welfare. You're gonna have to go down the Department of Public Welfare, and they'll tell you how you get Aid to Families with Dependent Children, which is a federal program. And then you can apply for medical assistance and food stamps from the state. But that's gonna take time, that's not gonna happen overnight. And the hospital is definitely *not* gonna let you camp out here in the waiting room. They *will* have their security people put you out, I guarantee it. So, what I'm tellin' you this for, is I really ought to talk to your father, let him know what's goin' on, explain all the options to him."

"You can't explain anything to him, you—"

"Just tell me what his name is and his number, okay? Let me worry about what I can explain to him."

It took nearly five more minutes of coaxing from both of

them before the girl would give her name, her father's name, and his phone number. She relented at last, shaking her head and saying, "It's just going to make him madder."

Balzic set off in search of a pay phone, relieved to have something to take his mind off his mother and his fear and to have someone on whom he could pour his anger. He was definitely looking forward to calling the father of the young mother.

A man answered on the third ring.

"Mister Zentner?"

"Yes. Who is this?"

"My name's Mario Balzic. I'm chief of police in Rocksburg. My wife and I have been talking to your daughter in the waiting room up here, in Conemaugh General Hospital?"

"What's she doing there?"

"What she's doing here is tryin' to camp out. And what I've been doin' for the last ten minutes or so is tellin' her that she can't do that, the hospital won't allow it. So, I explained, in a general way, what her welfare options are, but no matter what she decides to do, it's gonna take time. Nothin' moves slower than welfare, so I told her that the best place for her was back home with you—"

"She's not living here with me anymore. I made up my mind about that today. What she did was a sin. And I will not have that in my house."

"Well, I'm sure you think you won't, but I'm also sure you haven't given it enough thought."

"What? What are you talking about?"

"See, Mister Zentner, I've explained your daughter's options to her, and now I'm gonna explain your options to you."

"There aren't any options. Not where the word of God is concerned. 'Thou shalt not commit adultery.' There's no options there."

"Right. Absolutely right. But when it comes to the law, there's always lots of options. For example, Mister Zentner, you put your daughter on the streets of this city with no money, no food, no clothes except the clothes your child and her child were wearing, and no diapers, and not even a bottle. Mister Zentner, in my opinion, as a police officer, I believe that behavior constitutes endangering the welfare of children and the willful nonsupport of children. How old is your daughter?"

There was no answer.

"Mister Zentner? You hear me? How old is your daughter?"

After much clearing of his throat, Zentner said, "Seventeen."

"Then I won't have any trouble proving those charges against you. But I wanna tell you about another option. I want you to pay close attention to this. If you aren't down here in half an hour and pick up your daughter and take her home and keep her there until she gets straight with the welfare people—you listening?"

"Yes."

"If you don't come down here and get your daughter, I'm gonna arrest you, you stiff-necked sonofabitch and I'm gonna charge you with incest—"

"What? What did you say?"

"You heard me. With incest. And I'm gonna call every goddamn newspaper in the county and tell 'em about it when I do it. So you get your ass down here, you self-righteous prick, and take your daughter home or you're gonna spend the next couple of years explainin' to all your neighbors that your daughter's kid isn't yours, you follow me?"

There was no sound for a moment. Then there was an explosion. "That's a lie! That's a lie!"

"You either pick your daughter up in the next half hour, or you spend the next couple years tellin' your neighbors and your relatives—includin' your wife—why it is a lie."

"This is outrageous! This is—I'll sue! I'll sue you for slander! For defaming my character!"

"Mister, whatever you plan to do to me because of what I do to you—you payin' attention here?—whatever you plan to do to get even with me will not change what I do to you. Won't matter. All I have to do is go down to the judge who presides over Family Court and tell him that you put your seventeen-year-old daughter and her one-month-old child on the street without a change of clothes, with no money, and not even a bottle of water for your own granddaughter, and I guarantee you'll be sittin' in the county jail four, five months from now wonderin' what the fuck happened to your life. 'Cause I guarantee it, Mister Zentner, if you don't pick up those two children and take 'em home thirty minutes after I hang up, I guarantee that life as you know it will be over."

"I have—I have God on my side."

Balzic snorted. "You got thirty minutes on your side. You ain't here in thirty minutes, you're gonna need a lot more than God. You're gonna need a real sharp lawyer and a real deep pile of money. Bye."

As soon as he hung up, Balzic began to think about his mother. He ambled back down the corridor toward the waiting room, and all he could think about was his mother cooking, cleaning, dusting, washing clothes—working, always working. Only she never called it "working." She never called it anything other than what it was. She cooked, she cleaned, she did everything to keep them together, warm, dry, and fed, and she never said it was work. It was what it was, which was whatever was necessary to keep them warm, dry, and fed.

"What are you doing?"

"Baking." "Cleaning." "Making sauce."

"What kind?"

"Marinara. I got these beautiful tomatoes from Mister Cercone."

She never used the word *working*. Was he right about that? Was that true? Or was this another thing like the nun going down and out? Did he really remember that she never used the word *working*? "Ah, shit," he said aloud. "What does it matter?"

"I beg your pardon," a woman in white said, swiveling around as she passed him. "You talking to me?"

"Nah, nah," Balzic said, holding up his left hand and waving her off.

Ruth was standing, peering expectantly up the corridor at him.

"Brad said we may as well go. They just took her up and it'll be hours before he knows anything and we can see her. I could really go for a glass of wine. A sandwich. Wanna go home?"

"I don't know. Yeah. Sure, let's go."

Balzic stopped in front of the young mother. He handed her a card with his name and the number of the station on it. "If your father doesn't come to get you in a half hour, call this number."

He took Ruth's arm, and they walked out in silence to the car. He put the key in the ignition, looked over at her, and they fell together, awkwardly, sobbing, trying not to sob, trying to reassure each other and knowing their reassurances were the cheapest kind of lies: they were easy.

$$* \quad * \quad * \quad * \quad *$$

At home, on the deck at the rear of the house, Balzic walked from rail to rail, looking at the tomatoes and basil in the clay pots, bending over to smell one of the basil plants—the tallest one, the one with the white flowers smaller than the eraser on a pencil. Ruth came out with a plate of bread, provolone, roasted red peppers, marinated artichoke hearts, and black olives.

"It's good cheese," Balzic said. "Where'd you get it?"

"Conemaugh Importing."

He grunted appreciatively.

"Mar, we have to talk about some things."

He shook his head. "I don't wanna talk about any of those things we have to talk about."

"We're going to have to talk about it sooner or later."

"Then let's make it later."

"Mar, don't talk like that to me."

"Well don't talk like that to me either. I don't wanna talk about this shit now. 'Cause I know where this kind of shit talk goes. It goes to decidin' what kind of clothes we take to the funeral home and I'll be goddamned if I wanna talk about that now."

"Mario, we have never even talked about which funeral home we're going to call, and we can't put that off to the time when we're forced to make a decision. We ought to decide that now, when we aren't cryin'."

Balzic sighed. "I wouldn't let another human being but Sal Bruno touch her."

"Okay. I agree. So that's a big decision we just made."

"Swell. Do we win somethin'?"

"Mario, goddammit, she's your mother but she is *my best*

25

friend. If you think this is easier for me 'cause she's *your mother,* you're fulla shit. Eat some more and think! Think like you're helping *your* best friend help *her* best friend. And stop with the goddamn snide stuff."

"Jesus Christ, take it, ah. . . . She help you plant this stuff this year?"

Ruth shrugged. "The only thing she didn't help me with was watering. Bucket's too heavy for her. But then I got her that little plastic spout over there. By the rail. She uses that. . . . God I remember the first time she taught me how to make pesto. You know how long ago that was? Way before food processors. We did it with a mortar and pestle. I used the pestle and she poured the oil. I didn't even know what pesto was. I tried to fake like I knew, but as soon as she saw me tryin' to fake it, she knew. And I can't explain how she did it, but she showed me every step of the way and she never made me feel dumb. And I knew she knew I didn't know what the hell I was doin'. . . . That's when I wished she was my mother and I knew if I married you she would be my mother. I never told you that, did I?"

He snorted and laughed. "Ruth, you told me that the day after I proposed to you."

"I did?"

"And every anniversary."

"Really? You're makin' this up. Just to get even for about the nun."

"Had you goin' there for a second, didn't I?"

The phone rang then, and Balzic sighed and shrugged at Ruth and went inside to answer it. It was Stramsky.

"Yeah, Vic, what's up?"

"We got a body. Male. Many knife wounds. Out behind the porn store."

"Well, you know the drill. Listen, I won't be down there for fifteen, twenty minutes. I got to get something to eat."

"Sure. So how's your mother?"

"Doesn't look good. But they just started to run all the tests when we left. Right now, they think she had a stroke. We won't know for sure for a couple of hours, longer."

"Sorry to hear that, Mario. Your mom's one of the good guys."

"Yeah. She is. Thank you. So, d'you call everybody?"

"Listen, I called everybody. Take your time. We got it covered. They're either there or on their way."

"Okay. Where was it again? Behind the porn store?"

"Uh, apparently forty, fifty feet behind the store, in some trees."

Balzic acknowledged that and hung up. He went back out to the deck and found Ruth leaning against the rail, sipping wine between sobs.

He put his hands on her shoulders and kissed the back of her head.

"We had so much fun today . . . we were just talkin' and waterin' and sitting in the sun and . . . I was reading to her and she was telling me how . . . how all these clay pots made her feel so good 'cause they came from Italy and she could just look at them and they made her feel like she was home . . . and she told me how her mother used to make pasta and she had to carry it on a stick and hang it between two chairs to dry . . . she told me about their little yard between the houses, how the bricks were the same color as those pots and she used to make sure the chickens didn't get out into the road or the neighbors would steal their eggs, and sometimes the chickens . . . and she was so—she looked so content telling me about that. . . . Jesus, this was one of the best days she'd had in weeks. . . ."

"I know, I know," he said, knowing only that he didn't know. Those two words—"I know"—had such a ring of commiseration that it was almost impossible to not say them, even when only liars, drunks, or fools actually believed them. At times like this, who didn't want to believe that you knew?

"Sunshine enemas," he said, sighing.

"What?" She twisted around to look at him. "What did you say?"

"I was just givin' myself a sunshine enema. Hold my breath, pump the good news up there, then run for the can, and crap all the bad news and blues away."

"The blues? What blues? Since when did you start using

27

words like that? I never heard you use that word before. Since when did you start using that word? You were looking at that harmonica book, weren't you? What was it—*Zen and the Art of Blues Harp*? Was that it?"

"You caught me."

"Why didn't you get it, if you wanted it?"

"I feel stupid—I felt stupid."

"I think you ought to go back and buy it."

"I think what I better do is go see about this guy who got himself dead."

"Oh hell, Mario, let somebody else worry about that for once."

"Ruth, if I stay here I'm only gonna get drunk and start to blubberin' and feelin' sorry for myself."

"Then how 'bout staying here and making sure I don't get drunk and fall off the deck. Maybe I'd like some—never mind."

"Ruth, if I go, I won't have to think about her—"

"Mario, *if* you go nothing. *When* you go you'll be thinking about you. And I'll be here and I won't have any goddamn investigation to do to take my mind off anything. And I don't care who got himself dead. People have been getting dead long before I was born and they're going to be doing it long after I'm dead and tonight—oh shit, go on." She squirmed around him and walked to the opposite railing.

He closed his eyes and held up his hands and then let them drop. But he turned and went for the kitchen door, saying "So long" over his shoulder without looking back.

* * * * *

The porn store used to be a tire dealership. A sign proclaiming that fact was still standing, several of its letters missing: ROCKSTIRES in white letters on a blue background appeared above ALL   EASON   ADIALS $29.95 AND   P. Next to that sign was a new one: ADULT BOOKS TOYS NOVELTIES. MUST BE 21.

The large plate-glass windows were covered with plywood, as were the four bay doors. The only real window in the place seemed to be a small, diamond-shaped one in the entrance door.

A state-police laboratory van was parked next to a state-police cruiser. They were both near the end of the building. Parked by the front door was a Rocksburg PD cruiser. There were two other cars, one of which Balzic recognized as belonging to the coroner. He guessed the other one probably belonged to an assistant DA.

He parked near the lab van and got out, sizing up the place. It was very close to the Westfield Township border with Rocksburg, on the main state route leading to U.S. Route 22. He wondered where the employees' cars were parked, the customers'. Most likely, the sight of all these police vehicles was scaring off customers, though that didn't explain about the employees' cars.

He went around the side of the building and saw the cluster of men off in a dense copse of trees, twenty-five to thirty yards from the corner of the building. He also saw three cars parked against the rear wall of the building. A dumpster, with one of its two lids up, angled away from the rear wall on the far side of the last of the three cars.

Coroner Wallace Grimes picked his way carefully over the brush in the failing light.

Balzic waited for him. "Hi, Doc. How goes it?"

"Hello, Mario. Not very well for that young man. This is an ugly one. I quit counting wounds after I got to twenty-five. All puncture wounds with a fairly broad blade. A hunting knife is my first guess. Four in the genital area. No attempt to dismember. No slashing wounds. All puncture."

"What's he look like?"

"Young, late twenties I'd say. Small, smooth hands, clean fingernails, definitely not involved with physical labor, not a mechanic. Five-eight, five-nine, hundred and thirty, forty pounds. I think the state people have ID'd him; you'll have to check."

"Uh, the knifer definitely upset, huh?"

"Very. Great emotion at work there."

"Try to protect himself?"

"Oh yes. Many defensive wounds. He struck no blows. Just

29

tried to ward them off. Or if he did strike out, he certainly didn't make contact—not with his hands anyway."

"So whatta you think?"

"Off the record? No chance of having to repeat this?"

"Hey, Doc, it's just me."

"I'd say he was homosexual and he made a very big mistake. And I'd say the knifer is very angry about that sort of thing. Beyond that, which is way beyond what I'm supposed to be doing, I'm not going to speculate any further. Mario, I have to go. I left my wife at a neighbor's party and she really can't stand anybody there. She's not going to forgive me if I don't rescue her soon. Good night."

Balzic said good night and made his way carefully through the trees and over the thick brush to a small clearing, no more than ten or twelve feet square. He did not recognize any of the three state troopers, one with a camera, one with a flashlight walking bent over near the far side of the clearing, and one going through the contents of a wallet with a man in a sweat-stained running suit and shoes. They both turned to confront Balzic at the same time. He held up his ID case for them. He wondered who was driving the Rocksburg cruiser and where he was.

The man in the running clothes held out his hand. "Chief, I'm glad to meet you. I'm Ray David. I'm the new low man in the DA's office. This is Trooper Schieb."

Balzic shook hands with both and said, "Who is he?" He pointed at the body.

Schieb said, "Good question. He's got two different IDs, operator's licenses, Social Security, bank cards, health-insurance cards—he's got one for Blue Cross and he's got another one for Aetna. Also apparently had two vehicles, one registered in one name, and the other one in his other name. Just checked it out with BMV."

"Beg pardon?" Ray David said. "Checked it with who?"

"Bureau of Motor Vehicles computer, sir. BMV."

"Oh. And they said he had two cars?"

"Two cars, two insurance companies."

"What addresses?" Balzic said.

"One of 'em's here in Rocksburg. Uh, lemme see, 138

Roosevelt Way, Rocksburg Terrace. The other one's in Pittsburgh. On Walnut Street, Shadyside."

"How do you know that?" David said.

"Huh? Oh, I just got transferred from Washington Boulevard Barracks. I pulled a lot of heavy duty on Walnut Street."

"I thought that would be the city of Pittsburgh police, wouldn't it?"

"Yes, sir," Schieb said. "I was talking about recreation and rehabilitation, sir. I wasn't talking about pulling actual duty."

"Oh."

"What name's he got on the Rocksburg license?"

"Uh, Louis, L-O-U-I-S, Martin, Blaskevich, B-L-A-S-K-E-V-I-C-H."

"What's on the Pittsburgh license?"

"B-period-Lewis, L-E-W-I-S, Martin."

"Found any next of kin yet?"

"No, sir. We're not ready to do that yet. You wanna do it?"

"Well I don't want to do it, but I will." Only then did Balzic allow himself to look at the body. Louis Martin Blaskevich, AKA. B. Lewis Martin, was on his back with his arms crossed on his chest and his legs crossed at the ankles, his eyelids nearly closed, his soft, puffy face almost serene. "Jesus Christ . . ."

There was not a square inch of Louis Martin Blaskevich or B. Lewis Martin's shirt that wasn't soaked with blood. Balzic counted six wounds in the left side of the throat. Then he quit counting and turned his back on the body.

"Find a weapon?"

"Yes, sir," Trooper Schieb said. "It's in the lab van. It's a folding knife, about a four-inch blade. It's going to be real hard to track down. There are zillions of these damn things. Everybody sells 'em. My father has one just like it, so does my brother, my brother-in-law. Know the kind I mean?"

"Yeah, 'fraid so. Probably got a dozen of 'em in the property room right now. Anything else I oughta know before I go lookin' for his next of kin?"

"Yes, sir. Robbery was definitely not the main attraction here. He had one hundred and fifty-three dollars in bills, eighty cents in change, and four plastic cards, one for Rocksburg Savings and Loan, a MasterCard, a VISA, and an American Express."

"Anything else?"

"He also had about two ounces of pot in a Baggie in his back pocket, no seeds, no stems. I almost got buzzed just smellin' it. And those clothes are Calvin Klein's jeans and shirt. Those shoes—I remember pricin' a pair of those. That's one of the most expensive runnin' shoes you can buy. Almost a hundred bucks for those little sneaks there. About twice what I can afford."

"So? What else?"

"That aftershave he's wearin'? That's Pierre Cardin. See that red car over there? Next to the dumpster? That's an '85 BMW. Base price on that sucker's twenty-two big ones. The other owner's card he's got is for a Chevy Blazer, four-wheel drive, base price probably fifteen. This was one rich little fag here."

"I don't think we ought to be so quick to be making that kind of judgment," David said, his voice cracking.

"I'm not making a judgment, sir," Schieb said. "Just making an observation."

"Well I think you ought to keep those kind of observations to yourself." David was still having trouble controlling his voice.

"Whatever you say, sir," Schieb said evenly.

"Uh, anybody interviewin' the hired help?"

"Tried that, Chief. Not much there. The hired help's not gonna tell us a whole lot. Too scared."

"Why's that?" David piped up, indignant that something wasn't going according to the way he thought things should be going. "Was he told about what could happen to him for withholding information?"

"Uh, sir, do you know who owns this place?"

"No I do not, but what difference does that—"

"This place is owned by Leo Buckles and his son, Little Leo. Leo's six-four, about two-sixty. Little Leo's about six-six, two-seventy-five. Leo Senior is one of the smartest guys I ever met, but he has the morals of a tapeworm. Little Leo, if anything, isn't as finely tuned morally as his old man, plus he has the brains of a paper towel. In other words, sir, the hired help isn't really too interested in the more subtle points of the law regarding withholding information. He's not going to say anything until he gets an okay from Leo Senior."

32

"How do you know this Buckles?" Balzic said.

"Before I was at Washington Boulevard, I worked vice in Harrisburg. Leo's got five of these stores—this one here makes number six—from here to Harrisburg. I've known Leo for many years. All these stores are incorporated in his girlfriends' names. He's got a real sharp accountant; he pays all his taxes in full and on time. Since he got into this business, I guess he hasn't spent a whole day inside. Maybe. Maybe twenty-four hours total, but I doubt it."

"Uh-huh. Well you got a number for him?"

"Yeah, I think. Haven't called him in a while."

"Call him. Tell him what's happenin', tell him he needs to tell his clerk to do his duty."

"Or what?"

"Or—lemme see—or this place has a fire of suspicious origin, with the loss of the building and all its contents."

Assistant DA David sucked in his breath and his head spun. He fixed his gaze on Balzic. "Did I hear you right?" Even in the rushing loss of daylight, Balzic could see that David was suffering an acute attack of FOS: fear, outrage, and shock.

"I was just makin' a little joke," Balzic said.

"Well it wasn't very funny. My god, somebody overhear that, good night; they'd think that's the way we operate. And *that* is definitely *not* the way we operate—not on my cases we don't."

Balzic exchanged sidelong glances with Schieb. He waited until David turned away, then motioned to Schieb to follow him. Then Balzic stepped off cautiously through the brush into the parking lot and over to the red BMW near the dumpster. Schieb was only two steps behind.

"That klutz isn't gonna give us much time. You got the keys for this?"

"Yeah. Right here. Why?"

"Just open it and get in and pretend you're tossin' it again. You have tossed it, haven't you?"

"No, not yet."

"Then good. We'll do two things at once."

Inside the car, Balzic, feeling around the sun visor, said, "You, uh, call this Buckles and you tell him who I am and what I said. Tell him I never heard of this place 'til last week, and today some preacher walked in and gave me a headache about this place and tonight I got another headache. You do this for me and in return I will deliver the bad news to the next of kin, if there are any. Deal?"

"Fine with me. Watch it. Here comes Mister Sunshine Goodness. So, uh, d'you find anything on your side?"

"Nothing," Balzic said, and then his little finger struck something hard under the seat. "What's this?" He groped and grabbed and finally tugged out a large automatic pistol. "I'll be goddamned," he said. "Look at this. Turn the light on—or open the door."

Schieb fumbled for the overhead light switch and turned it on. "Now that's a surprise, man. I would've bet that if this little faggot had a gun, it would've been a cute little .25 auto or maybe a pearl-handled stainless steel .32. I would've bet a hundred bucks, if he did have a gun, it wouldn't be one like that."

Balzic was holding it up, turning it this way and that to try to read what it was. "You know this piece?"

"Sure do. Got one. That's a Beretta 9mm. U.S. Government just bought about three hundred of those. That's a fine weapon there. Man, I shoot three-inch groups at twenty-five yards with that machine. One handed. And I'm not that good. At ten yards? I can put five of 'em in there you can cover with a silver dollar. Wonder what this little faggot was into?"

Schieb was rummaging through the glove box. "Look at this, look at this." He held up a Baggie filled with white powder. "So now we know how he paid for his two cars. Man, I wonder what other treasures we're gonna find here."

David appeared at the window and rapped on it.

Balzic tried to wind the window down but gave up after he couldn't find a handle. "This thing must be all power."

"All power?" Schieb said. "Shit, this thing'll do everything but fuck and figure out your income tax."

Balzic opened the door finally, allowing David to lean in. "Anything new?"

"Well, we're finding out that our victim had a well-rounded personality. He wasn't just a one-dimensional fairy."

David stiffened and, his voice cracking again, said, "Trooper,

I admonish you to stop making such comments. I'm not going to warn you again."

"Yes, sir. Won't happen again."

"So what have you found?"

"We've found a 9mm pistol and a Baggie with a lot of white powder in it. But I'm making no assumption from that. It's possible that these two items could have been placed in this vehicle by the perpetrator in an attempt to give us a false picture of the victim's life-style and cause us to waste valuable time speculating about them, which the perpetrator would use to make good his escape."

Balzic had to bite the inside of his lower lip to keep from laughing, but David was not amused.

"Trooper, what *is* your problem?"

"Uh, my problem, sir? My problem is I'm six months from retirement, sir, and I'm the same rank now as I was when I graduated from the academy. That's my problem."

"I don't know what you're talking about."

"Of course you don't, sir, because you're—"

"I think it's time for me talk to the family," Balzic said as loudly as he could without shouting, trying to cut Schieb off. "C'mon, Mr. DA David, you wanna go meet the family?" Balzic got out of the BMW and tried to steer David by the arm away from further conversation with Schieb, but David pulled back.

"I want to hear what his problem is."

"Aaaah, his problem, his problem. His problem is he's overworked and underpaid. Then he has to come to work and look at things like we've just been lookin' at and he gets a little testy, a little salty around the edges, and then he thinks, hell, he's seen some people make lieutenant, captain even, and he can't understand why he never made corporal, so he tends to get a little bitter, a little resentful, a little hostile, and he tends to say things he wishes he hadn't, that's all his problem is, it's no big deal here. So the rest of us should be a little more understanding, we shouldn't make a big deal out of it, if you follow me."

David drew his head back and squinted at Balzic. "You the chief of police or the chairman of the local Democratic Party?"

Balzic laughed softly and patted David on the shoulder. "My

wife sometimes—especially when she's real real mad—calls me a 'silver-tongued bastard.' But of course she loves me, so she can be expected to say something like that. Uh, why don't we walk over here awhile?"

"What for?"

"So you can tell me how long you've been with the DA's office, and so I can talk to you like you're my nephew."

David bristled. "I don't need any new relatives. My family's all full. And how long I've been with the office does not seem to me to be a fit subject for your investigation."

Balzic looked at his shoes for a moment, and then looked into David's lean, flushed face. "Well then. Since you're such a veteran of this sort of thing, I'll leave it to you to inform the next of kin that a member of their family has died in a real ugly way, that he had two identities, and that an unlicensed weapon and illegal drugs were found in his vehicle. And I'm sure you'll be able to observe their reactions and remember their answers to your questions while you're doin' it. Good night."

Balzic turned abruptly and set off for his car. He had not taken three steps before David called out to him to stop. But Balzic didn't. Fuck you, he thought.

"Wait a second," David said, nearly breaking into a run to catch up. "Wait a second." He pulled even with Balzic and grabbed his arm.

Balzic jerked his arm away, stumbled on some gravel, and, nearly losing his balance, he thrust his index finger in David's face. "I don't know what the fuck your job description is, mister, but I know what mine is and mine says nobody puts their goddamn hands on me. Your family's all full up? Huh? Well my mother's in the goddamn hospital right now and I don't know whether she's gonna be alive tomorrow and I'm standin' here listenin' to some—ahhhhh, how many cases you ever prosecute, huh?"

David hung his head. "This . . . this is my first."

"Yeah, uh-ha. Well, first rule is this, kid. Don't ever grab this chief of police. 'Cause you make that mistake again, this chief's gonna kick you in your private parts so hard that next time you take a piss it's gonna be through your nose."

David continued to hang his head. Then he brought his chin

up and said softly, "Just because I'm new at this doesn't mean you can threaten me. I don't believe I deserve that."

"Kid, if I wanted to put you in the emergency room, I wouldn't've made a speech first. I'd've just done it. So don't go pickin' nits with me."

David tried not to glare. He wanted to glare—that was obvious—but he also seemed to know that he should be showing a lot less macho and a lot more respect. He was just having trouble finding the right face to put on.

"What is your problem anyway?"

"I just happen to believe that law officers should not be making prejudicial statements."

"Prejudicial statements? About what?"

"About the victim's life-style."

Balzic tried to comprehend that. "You pissed because that trooper called the victim a fag?"

"Yes, I am."

"Jesus Christ why?"

"I think it's a clear indication the investigating officer has already lost his objectivity."

Balzic poked his glasses up his nose and mulled that one over. "Uh, this your first job, kid? You brand new?"

"This is my first job, yes."

"Uh-ha. Well, kid, that objectivity stuff—and remember now, I never went to law school, never went to college—but a friend of mine, I've heard him call that 'objectivity' one of our myths. And he'd say a myth was somethin' everybody professed to believe in but was somethin' nobody no way in hell could live up to. I heard him talkin' about this one day, and he said, objectivity's fine as long as you remember there's just as much goin' on behind you as there is in front of you but your eyes are only in the front of your head, and no matter how fast you try to turn around, your eyes are always only in the front of your head."

"I'm sure there's a point, but I—"

"The point, kid, is you can be objective as hell, but if you're lookin' in the wrong direction, what the hell good's your objectivity doin' you?" Balzic canted his head to try to read

David's face, to see if what he was saying was making any impression. "Don't get it yet, do you?"

"I'm trying. But I still don't see how what you're saying mitigates what the trooper said about the victim."

"What I'm sayin' is, just because the trooper made what sounded to you like a prejudiced remark doesn't mean he's gonna go to sleep during the rest of his investigation. You're confusin' the issue. You're confusin' what the trooper said with what he's gonna do. Besides which, if you can look at the victim, where he is, what he looks like, how he's dressed, and so forth, and not know that he was a fag, then *you're* the one who's lettin' his prejudices get in the way of his common sense. 'Cause everything about that body says fag. And that's what the trooper was sayin': he was makin' an observation, not a judgment."

Balzic shrugged and sighed. "What's it gonna be, kid? You gonna stay here and debate, or you wanna go see the next of kin? You wanna see 'em by yourself or you wanna watch me while I do it, see how it's done?"

"I suppose I should go with you."

Balzic nodded and led the way to his cruiser.

* * * * *

Rocksburg Terrace sat on the plateau of Rocksburg's highest hill. The Terrace was a cluster of wood apartment houses with flat roofs that had been built during World War II to house Mexican laborers who had been brought in by the federal government to build LSTs, Landing Ship Tanks, at the Conemaugh Boat Works.

"I remember how pissed all the hunkies were," Balzic said to David as they drove along the narrow streets looking for 138 Roosevelt Way.

"Why? About the Mexicans?"

"Yeah. They still had the Depression in their throats, I guess. Couldn't understand how all these goddamn Mexicans had to be brought in here, get jobs for good pay, and then the government builds these apartments for 'em, and just a couple years before the government wasn't doin' a damn thing for anybody. Not only weren't they buildin' places for people to live, banks were closin' on everybody and the government was standin' there with a gun makin' sure there was no argument. That had to be pretty hard to take. I don't know. I just remember hearin' guys talkin' about burnin' this place down. Course it's obvious nobody did. I mean they're still here. Course the guys doin' most of the talkin' were the 4-F'ers, so maybe they were just lookin' for somebody to fight. Here we go: 138 Roosevelt Way."

"How . . . how do you do this?"

"How do you do what?"

"How do you tell—how do you say it?"

"I don't know. I don't plan it. I used to. Used to rehearse like crazy. Then one day I told a guy his kid was dead and he started laughin'. He said somethin' like, 'It's about time,' or somethin' like that. Ever since then, I just go with who opens the door and how they look and hope I'm right."

"You mean you really don't know what you're going to say until they open the door?"

"Yeah. I mean, they know something's up as soon as I show my ID and ask 'em if I can come in and if they wanna sit down. They know I'm not there to sell 'em aluminum siding."

"I don't know," David said, looking himself up and down after he got out of the cruiser. "All of a sudden, I think I look ridiculous. I mean, trying to tell somebody that—jeez, look at me. And my god I stink. Whew! Maybe I should stay here."

"Hey, whatever," Balzic said. "But you won't learn anything out here." He set off down the narrow, cracked concrete path. He had to step around two light-skinned black kids, ages four or five, who were digging in the patchy grass.

Each building housed four apartments, and he was heading for the end apartment. The night was suddenly taking on a chill. He turned and glanced back at the two black kids. Both were wearing shorts and sleeveless shirts, but they were oblivious to the weather. Balzic turned back and nearly collided with a short, pudgy white woman, her straight brownish hair stringy in the breeze. She wore rubber thongs, and they flopped as she shuffled along the wall toward the two black kids, calling out to them, telling them she wasn't going to call them to come inside again. They ignored her and continued to dig.

Balzic reached the door marked 138 and pushed the bell and rapped on the aluminum storm door. He got no answer, but before he could knock again, David had arrived, looking confused and sheepish.

Balzic hit the bell and knocked again, louder. He could hear a TV playing inside and he could see it flickering through a window to his left. He pounded on the door with the flat of his hand.

The inner door opened a sliver. Balzic held his ID case close to the sliver. "This the Blaskevich residence?"

The door closed, then opened after the chain lock was undone. The only light inside was coming from the TV screen.

"What's the matter?" came a phlegmy voice. It was hard to tell whether it was male or female.

"May we come in? I'm Mario Balzic, chief of police here, and this is Assistant District Attorney Ray David."

"What for?"

"May we come in, please? I have an unpleasant duty to perform and I'd rather do it inside, please?"

The door opened slowly and Balzic led David in. They stopped just inside and waited while their eyes adjusted to the dark.

"Would you turn on a light, please?" Balzic said. About that time he smelled a heavy breeze of whiskey, followed immediately by an explosion of phlegmy coughing, which was followed immediately by the bright glare of a bare bulb directly overhead. Balzic's eyes shot downward reflexively and he held his gaze to the floor for a moment, then he turned to see purple wedgies, bare feet, ankles, shins, and calves a mass of broken veins. His eyes went up a yellowish, shapeless cotton housedress covered with a nondescript floral print. Bare arms and hands looked like the feet and calves. The face was a lumpy mass; there seemed to be no definition to any of its parts. What struck Balzic was the size of the woman's earlobes, bigger than a penny, and the garish orange color of her unruly hair. Her eyelids were so puffy Balzic could not have guessed the color of her eyes. Her lips were working involuntarily, as though she was whispering. She gazed at Balzic drunkenly, and she stumbled as she pointed toward an arch leading into the room where the TV was playing.

Balzic stepped through the arch and took only two steps into the room. He was having a hard time adjusting to the loss of light again. Then he heard the woman shuffle woozily around him and David and heard the click of a table lamp.

"Got a smoke?" she said.

"No, ma'am."

"How 'bout you?" she said, eyeing David crookedly.

"I don't smoke."

"Don't care if you do," she snapped. "Didn't ast you if you did. Ast you if you had one."

"No, I don't."

"Then I gotta get one. Mine's in the kitchen. Be right back, next week maybe."

She staggered out through the arch and disappeared. She was gone for what seemed a minute, scraping chairs around, opening and closing drawers. Then came the sound of garbage being dumped on the floor.

"Oh shit," Balzic said. He turned to David and said, "Go find some cigarettes or we're gonna be here forever."

"Where am I going to find cigarettes? I don't even know where I am. I'm in these ridiculous clothes, I don't have any money."

"Uh, apparently you didn't learn this in law school, but a DA prosecutes a case by askin' questions. So go outside and ask people if you can mooch some cigarettes."

"Gawwwd, this is . . . this is absurd."

"Not half as absurd as what we're gonna be doin' if you don't find some new cigarettes, 'cause this woman is rootin' through her garbage lookin' for a butt. You wanna mooch new cigarettes, or you wanna root through garbage? 'Cause we ain't gonna do nothin' here until this woman gets somethin' to smoke."

"Well what're you going to do while I'm doing this?"

"Whatta you think? I'm gonna hunt for a butt for her, or would you rather do that and I'll go try to mooch some, huh? Which?"

"Oh, gawd, I'll go outside, never mind."

Uh-hm, Balzic thought. Hope you have brains enough to be polite. Don't wanna have to run you back to the hospital.

He went out to the tiny kitchen and found the woman on her knees, sifting through her garbage. To her right she had laid out five butts, none more than an inch long.

"Want some help?"

"I know there's a long one in here. Only took two drags on it. But maybe that was yesterday. 'Cept I think it was today."

Balzic got down on his knees and picked up an advertising flier and rolled it into a tube, and began to poke around with it. Surprisingly, the pile didn't smell as bad as he'd thought.

"Uh, listen, Momma, you Missus Blaskevich?"

"Listen who? I ain't your momma. Who are you anyway?"

"I'm the chief of police, remember? Balzic? You let me in a little while ago."

"Oh yeah. Course I let a lotta youns in. And youns never have any money and youns never have any ciggies."

"Uh-ha. Are you Missus Blaskevich?"

"Scheese. Sure. Why not? I been Toscarella, I been Hiteshue, I been Crivella, hell, sure I been Blaskevich."

"Were you Blaskevich first? Or last?"

"Lemme see—oooh, here's a good one. This is the one I was lookin' for. Look there. Only took couple drags off this one." She stood up with much grunting and wobbling, and wove her way over to a small gas stove, put the butt in her mouth, turned on one of the burners, and leaned over, touching butt to flame, being careful to hold back the hair on the side of her head nearest the gas. She stood up and exhaled smoke triumphantly. She tucked her chin back and said, "Ha! Sonofabitch said I couldn't do nothin'. Well I can find a goddamn butt when I have to. Pretty good, huh? Whatta you doin' down there? You don't have to clean that up. I'll do that tomorrow. I got all day, know what I mean? Giddup for crissake. Make me nervous down there. Look like you're gettin ready to kill bugs or somethin'. What the hell is it with guys, every time they see a bug they gotta kill it. Every time they see somethin' crawlin' they gotta step on it. Jesus Christ Almighty, I been crawlin' all my life, every sonofabitch comes in here sooner or later thinks it's his job to step on me, know what I mean? Who the hell are you anyway? We ever been introduced—formally, I mean?"

"Uh, Missus Blaskevich, you have a son?"

"A son? Yeah, every once in a while. Izzat what this is about? He—he got dead, isn't he? He's dead, huh?"

"Well, ma'am, what I want you to do is come with me to Conemaugh Hospital. I want you to look at somebody. I—it's gonna be hard, ma'am, because he was very badly injured, and it's not gonna be a very pleasant thing to look at. I wish you were in better shape, ma'am, but under the circumstances, maybe you're in the best shape you could be in. But I need to know whether this is your son or not."

"Lemme think a minute. Did he have two driver's licenses? Huh? With two different names? Was one of them like Louis Martin or somethin' like that?"

"Yes, ma'am."

"Then that was him. I don't need to look at him."

"Well, yes, ma'am, that's what his cards said. But, see, I need you to look at this person we found and tell us if this person is who's named on all the cards and plastic."

"He got stepped on, didn't he?"

"Yes, ma'am, I'm afraid he did."

"The sonsabitches always think you're crawlin' just 'cause you're on your knees, you know what I mean? The sonsabitches never believe you when you say you're lookin' for somethin', that's how come you're on your knees. Maybe what you want's down on the floor. They think everybody ain't lookin' for the top shelf oughta be stepped on, the bastards. Pricks . . . ya know what I mean? . . . Pricks . . . you know what I'm sayin'?"

David knocked on the door and stepped inside, smiling brightly. "Hey, I found a pack of Kools."

"Oh shit," Mrs. Blaskevich said. "I hate menthol."

*   *   *   *   *

In one respect, identifying the body was not as bad as Balzic had thought it might be; in another respect it was worse. Mrs. Blaskevich was drunk enough to be distracted: she looked at her son with a woozy kind of detachment that brought forth no more emotion than a series of long sighs, each followed by another request for a cigarette or a cup of coffee or both. The cigarettes and coffee were easy; despite all the no-smoking signs everywhere in the hospital, there was a cigarette machine in an employees' lounge two doors down from the pathology lab that served as morgue. Right next to the cigarette machine was a coffee machine. A positive identification of the victim cost Balzic a pack of Camels and two cups of coffee, extra cream, extra sugar.

What was worse was listening to Ray David bitch about the ingratitude of people who couldn't afford the luxury of turning down mentholated cigarettes. David followed Balzic to the employees' lounge every trip. His bitching was unrelenting.

Balzic's tongue found an upper molar. "Don't take this wrong, understand? But there are two facts you need to remember. One, the lady is a juicer. Two, the lady has just identified the victim of a goddamn ugly homicide as her son. What I've heard outta you every trip I've made into this room is this lady has some nerve turnin' up her nose at menthol cigarettes. What I haven't heard from you every time I've come in here is, here, let me pay for somethin'."

"I'm still in my running clothes, for crying out loud."

"You got a home?"

"A what? Of course I have a home. An apartment."

"You got clothes there?"

"Certainly."

"Then your problem is solved. You go home, you take those clothes off, you put other clothes on, you put money in the pockets, and you come back. And one more thing. This is very important. Somewhere between here and your place? Stick those menthol cigarettes up your ass, I don't wanna hear another word about 'em."

"I beg your pardon?"

"Don't beg nothin', okay? This is the world here. Nothin' works the way it's advertised, and nobody acts like you think they're supposed to. While you're followin' me around bitchin' about the way this woman reacted to those cigarettes, you haven't got one piece of information out of her."

"The woman's alcoholic, anybody can see that. What am I supposed to ask her?"

Balzic shrugged. "Don't ask her anything. Wait until everything's perfect. Wait until she gets back from a month dryin' out. Then wait three more weeks till she kicks nicotine. Then you put on your lightweight wool pinstripe and you find some red leather chairs, and a fireplace, and you two can have a nice little chat and straighten all this out. You know, like Missus Marple."

"Like who?"

"Give me a fucking break, will you? Go home."

Balzic left him standing there, his mouth pinched shut.

*　　*　　*　　*　　*

"Missus Blaskevich, you wanna tell me about your son?"

"No. I wanna go home. I wanna drink. I don't think there's anything at home to drink. You got a couple bucks you wanna loan me?"

"No, ma'am, I don't."

"Then you wanna take me somewhere and buy me a drink? Maybe a couple six-packs. I'll drink draft beer. I don't care. I ain't proud."

"Whatta you live on, ma'am? Social Security, welfare, what?"

"Social Security? Do I look sixty-five to you? You better get your glasses checked, buddy boy. I ain't no fogey yet."

"Yeah, uh-ha. What I mean is, what're you livin' on? Where's the money come from?"

"I have a husband."

"I'm sure you do. He's not your son's father, right?"

"Hell no. I can't even remember his father. Maybe he didn't have one. Maybe he was a virgin birth."

"Uh-ha. Did your son contribute to your support?"

"Sup-port? Support? My son didn't support nothing or nobody but his own goddamn self. Most selfish little brat that ever was." She turned her face toward Balzic and seemed to be staring at him, but he couldn't tell because her lids were so puffy.

"I had these big tits," she said. "And everybody was always

45

trying to grab me or feel me up or making wisecracks and I always pretended it made me mad but I was always kinda proud. Don't know why. I didn't do a goddamn thing to get 'em. But from the seventh grade on, everybody was looking at my tits and saying they wanted to do this and they wanted to do that. Then I had him. And . . . and I didn't have no milk. Goddamn kid almost starved to death and there I am putting my beautiful big tits in his mouth and he sucks and he sucks and I feel so . . . Jesus, I feel wonderful. And I take him off me and he starts crying right away and I don't know what the hell's going on. And after a week I take him back to the doctor and he tells me the kid's lost a pound and a half and he's starving to death. And he squeezes my tits and just this little dribble comes out. And I felt so goddamn useless. And I wanted to go get all the guys that ever grabbed me and say, 'Well, what do you think of me now, you sonsabitches? I got these great-lookin' tits and they don't work so what good are they? All they do is give you sonsabitches a hard-on but I can't even feed my own baby.' You know what I'm talking about?"

"I think."

"Who are you again?"

"Balzic. Rocksburg chief of police."

"I wanna go get a drink. Whatta ya say, big boy. Am I good for a drink?"

"Yeah, sure, why not. Ever been to Muscotti's?"

"Christ, who hasn't? You live in this town and you drink, sooner or later you wind up in Dom's. Gotta admit, I ain't been there in a long time. C'mon. Might be good for a laugh. Christ knows I could use a laugh about now. That was my kid in there, wasn't it?"

"I'm afraid it was."

"If I'd known he was going to wind up like that, I would've never took him back to the doctor's. I shoulda just let him keep suckin' on my tits. He would've died happy. He sure wasn't happy when he died. You ever see a mess like that?"

"No," Balzic lied. He'd seen plenty of them. Some a lot worse. "C'mon. Grab hold of my arm."

She rose unevenly out of the molded plastic chair and took

his arm. "I don't have—I can't afford no funeral, for god's sake. How am I going to do that?"

"Well we'll see what we can do. Watch your step."

*   *   *   *   *

Muscotti's was practically empty—Dom was behind the bar and a man and two young women were at one table—but the man was performing sleight of hand with coins to impress the young women and the three of them were making quite a ruckus, the women making all kinds of giggly appreciative noises.

Balzic led Mrs. Blaskevich gently but firmly down the back steps and to the last two seats at the bar, near the kitchen.

Dom sidled down the bar from the front, where he'd been staring out the windows, his thumbs flicking against his index fingers, and he stopped in front of the woman. He leaned on the bar and canted his head and scowled at her.

"What the hell you doin' here? Last time you were in here I told you get the hell out and never come back. You think I forgot that?"

"This wasn't my idea," she said, pointing three times with her thumb at Balzic. "He brought me."

Muscotti scowled at Balzic. "You losin' your mind or what? This one's in the Pain In The Ass Hall of Fame. She was elected unanimously."

"She just came from identifying her son in the morgue."

"Gimme a Chivas Regal and water. Twist of lemon."

"I'll give ya a twist all right. I'll twist your head off."

"Hey, whoa, Jesus, take it easy. I just told you where the woman came from. She wanted a drink. I brought her here. You got a problem with that, tell me about it."

"Yeah I got a problem with it. This bag here tried to put a squeeze on me. She got some friggin' idea in her head she wanted to be a showgirl in Vegas, she decided I was gonna be the one to pay for the trip. I told her I didn't owe her nothin'. She told me, I don't pay, she's gonna write a little letter to my wife. I didn't pay. And she did. Ain't that right, Mabel? Huh? And for a year after that I was in hell, that's where I was. My

47

wife knew me since she was eighteen and she believes a letter from some hustler she never met in her life." Dom leaned forward and his voice got lower. "You want a drink? How 'bout Corby's and water? You want a twista lemon? Go to Florida and pick one out. I'll twist it. I'll cut it and then I'll twist it. Which is what I shoulda done when my wife opened that letter from you. Better yet, what I shoulda done, you wanted to go to Vegas so bad, I shoulda sent you. I shoulda sent you to a couple guys I knew out there. You wanted to be a showgirl? They would've showed you all over Vegas.

"Mario, I can see from your face this is an honest mistake. But don't ever bring her in here again, I don't care how many times she goes to the morgue."

Balzic splayed his hands. "Hey, Dom, what can I say?"

"Don't say nothin'." He turned away, reached for a bottom-shelf bottle and a glass, quickly poured a shot into the glass and then filled it with water and slid it in front of Mrs. Blaskevich.

"Could I have some ice?"

"Every time you take a sip, think of my heart. I guarantee it'll be the coldest drink you ever tasted." Muscotti turned to Balzic. "What's it gonna be? Wine? Beer? What?"

"Beer. Draft."

Dom poured one and set it in front of Balzic. "That'll be twenty bucks."

"What?"

"Seventy-five cents for the beer, nineteen and a quarter for the whiskey and water."

"Are you shittin' me or what?"

"I ain't shittin' you, so I guess it's 'what.' Education's expensive. And nobody learns nothin' unless they remember the price."

"Jesus Christ," Balzic said, "I thought I was in a saloon for a while. Turns out I'm in the University of Pittsburgh, the goddamn Cathedral of Learning. You want twenty bucks? Huh? Put it on my tab."

"You ain't got a tab."

"What the hell're you talkin' about? I run a tab here for years. You losin' it or what?"

"Pennsylvania Liquor Code prohibits the sale of wine, beer, and spirits on credit. You know that as well as I do. Better."

"Oh for crissake. Little while ago you said I made an honest mistake."

"Yeah. I did. I also said if you never remember the price, you never learn. And I don't want you to forget this."

"Hey, guys. Could I have another one? Huh?"

"Jesus, you sure pounded that one down. What's this one gonna cost me?"

"I was always a nervous drinker. I drink fast when I'm nervous."

"Probably cost you the same as the last one."

"Aw will you stop for crissake."

"My wife ain't trusted me for forty years because of this *putan*. And in forty-five years I was unfaithful to my wife twice. And neither time was with her. Whatta you think that's worth? You think forty bucks—a dollar a year—you think that's too much to ask? Huh?"

"Hey, Dom. I didn't send the fuckin' letter, how come I'm payin'?"

"You're payin' 'cause you still don't understand how everything is."

"Jesus Christ. Next thing you'll be tellin' me is I gotta pay 'cause you weren't born a goddamn Rockefeller or a Mellon."

"Now that you mention it, it ain't such a bad idea."

"Can I get another one?"

"Shuddup," Balzic said. "Give her another drink and put it on my tab. And if you don't, I'll call the Liquor Control Board and tell 'em you been runnin' tabs in here for years and I'll be the lead-off witness against ya, how d'you like that, *paisan*?"

Muscotti smiled crookedly. "I always said you shoulda been president of the Teamsters."

"Yeah. You're adorable, too. But if my tab shows forty bucks on it, I will sic the LCB on your ass."

Muscotti shrugged grandly. "Hey, I just remembered—I'm havin' a sale. Two for one. Sale just started."

Muscotti refilled Mrs. Blaskevich's drink and drew another glass of beer for Balzic, at first as though nothing was out of the ordinary, but then he grew distracted and nervous.

49

Muscotti waited momentarily until Mrs. Blaskevich seemed to drift off, then he nodded for Balzic to follow him into the kitchen, a mere four steps from where Balzic had been standing.

"So?"

"So somebody really take her kid out?"

"Yeah. We just came from the morgue. Didn't I say that?"

Muscotti scratched his cheek, his glasses bouncing up and down. "He was with some heavy people, you know?"

"I don't know anything."

"Well he was."

"I'm listenin'."

"You don't know anything about him?"

"What did I just say?"

"I heard what you said."

Balzic sighed. "Hey, Dom, how long you known me?"

"Why you askin' me that?"

"Why you askin' me whether I knew anything about this guy after I told you I didn't know anything about him? What the fuck we doin' here?"

"I'm just real surprised you didn't know anything about him, that's all."

Balzic squeezed his nose with his thumb and index finger and exhaled at the same time, so that it sounded like somebody pulling an air hose off a tire valve when he took his hand away. "Dom, I hate these fuckin' conversations when you do this, how surprised you are I didn't know somebody after I just got through tellin' you I didn't know this somebody. So you wanna tell me somethin', then please tell me, okay?"

Muscotti mulled that over. "Okay. Her kid was tryin' to move up real fast. He started movin' up, then he turned into, uh, like, all the assholes who wanna be bad. You know. He started to run his mouth. Hey, Mario, there's only one thing worse, you know? He didn't buy a billboard that said, 'Hi. I'm so and so. Here's my phone number and this is where I live. I deal in illegal goods and services. Call me for a good time.' That's the only thing he didn't do. Otherwise," Muscotti said, holding up his hands slowly, "it was only a matter of time. I'm gonna be as straight as

I can. I don't know who did him. But I know who was gettin' ready to do him."

Balzic looked at the floor and then at Muscotti. "Jesus, I can't believe you're tellin' me this."

"Hey, Mario, what the hell you want? I'm tellin' you this *ciadrule* was in a jackpot, you're gonna ask for my motives? What the fuck."

Balzic blew out his breath. "I'm not askin' your motives. I'm just thinkin' about this whole scene. I'm the goddamn chief of police. You're who you are. Not ten feet away sits a lush whose son we're talkin' about as though he was a piece of shit. And he's dead. I just looked at him. He's deader'n shit."

"Hey, Mario," Dom said, touching Balzic lightly on the shoulder. "My mother says all the time, 'It don't matter who dies, somebody still gotta make dinner.' All I can add to that is, somebody still got to go downstairs and get the wine and bring it up and open it and pour it. I don't give a fuck who died. Somebody got to go get the wine, *cabeesh*?"

"Yeah. Okay. So who is this guy? So who was he doin' business with?"

"I don't know who. All I know is, somebody was gettin' ready to give him the big bye-bye. But whoever did this—how'd he get it again?"

"Knife."

"How with the knife—in and out?"

"Yeah."

"Lots of times?"

"Yeah."

"Definitely personal. Definitely a lefty. Joints are full of 'em. Definitely the weapon of choice. In and out. What am I tellin' you? You know this."

Balzic nodded slowly, licking his upper teeth. "She really write a letter to your wife?"

"You think I'd make somethin' like that up?"

"No."

"Then what the hell you want from me? An affidavit?"

"No no no, c'mon."

"Listen to me. Ever since my wife got that letter, I been two pounds of shit in a one-pound bag. And no matter how I explained it, I couldn't make my wife understand that broad was puttin' the arm on me. It was a scam. I never did nothin' with her. I can't tell you how many times I wanted to put her in three different garbage bags. But I never did. 'Cause I knew if I was in her place I'd have probably tried to work the same kind of hustle. I got sympathy, you understand? People think I don't, but I do. I mean, Jesus Christ, if I didn't, there'd be bodies scattered from here to Harrisburg. Jesus Christ, half the people I know'd be dead."

"So why don't you know who he was doin' business with?"

"You kiddin'?" Muscotti leaned close and peered intently into Balzic's eyes. "I'm a Mustache Pete. I'm a dinosaur. I'm history."

Balzic was incredulous. "Since when?"

"Since a while ago."

It was Balzic's turn to peer. He peered as hard as he could. It made no difference: He had no idea whether Muscotti was telling the truth or pulling his leg.

"You say 'a while ago,' but I haven't even heard a rumor about this. You puttin' me on?"

"I wish. You don't deal dope, you're a Mustache Pete. I seen it comin', I ain't completely stupid. In one way. In another way I'm stupider than stupid. I thought, hey, I'm here in the boonies, it'll be forever before they get around to me. That's when you know you're gettin' old, when you think with your ego. Thirty, thirty-five years ago, we said the same thing about other guys. They were too dumb to do anything but the old Black Hand things. Sellin' juice, cheesuz, what a bunch of smart asses we were, the original wiseguys, we knew all the places to park the money. All they wanted to do was import olive oil and pecorino. So I told 'em, nah, you guys don't understand; you gotta get the food, you gotta get the linen, and most of all, you gotta get the garbage." Muscotti stepped back to glance around the door into the bar.

"So they said I was nuts. But that's what I got. I got the sheets, the towels, the linen service at the hospital. I got the food in a bunch of schools. Half this county dumps garbage in my holes in my ground. And I lay off most of the action. So you'd think that would be good enough, right?" Muscotti snorted derisively.

"The guy that tells me, huh? He brings two bikers to my

house. He's twenty-six years old and he brings two bikers to my house. He brings 'em inside with him. He don't ask if it's okay if they come in, he don't ask nothin'. He walks 'em right past me. I look at him, he sits 'em down at my dining-room table. He don't say hello, kiss my ass, I'm the new chairman of the board, he don't say nothin' but 'You can keep your saloon, the dump, the hospital, and the food. You can keep ninety percent of it. You send us the rest.' Then they get up and leave. Little while later, I'm callin' around, I find out his old man is a guy I showed how to run a dice game. So I called him and I told him, tell his son never bring those bikers near my house again. You know what he tells me? 'I don't tell my son nothing. My son tells me.' I told him he must be nuts. He said, 'I ain't nuts, I'm just ignorant. I don't know where to get the white powder. And if you don't know where to get that, then you got to let the guys who do bring bikers into your house.' He said they were in his house all the time. And then he hung up on me. And I thought to myself, What is this respect shit I used to hear about all the time? Click. That's what it is. That's—"

"Hey, can anybody get a drink or youns gonna yuk it up all night?"

"Shuddup," Muscotti growled. "Where was I—oh. So I went to see somebody. I said, 'Is this the way it's done now?' He says, 'It's a new day. New faces, new places. It's a new day.' That's it. That's the whole conversation from his end. I said, 'All due respect, I been paying you since I was eighteen. This mean I have to keep paying you and pay him too?' He shakes his head yeah and he gets up and walks outta the room and leaves me standin' there. It takes me, I don't know, Christ, ten seconds to figure out he ain't coming back. All of a sudden, I get a whole new look at life. A whole new perspective. Walking outta there, it was like the floor was covered with marbles. It felt like it took me ten minutes to get from where I was standin' to the front door. It was fifteen, twenty feet. I was takin' these little shuffles, like some old guy, so I don't fall on the marbles, which ain't there of course." Muscotti closed his eyes and clenched his teeth and sighed heavily through his nose.

Balzic was trying to comprehend everything he'd been hearing. He could not remember when he had not known Dom

Muscotti, and not known who he was and what he did, but this was the first time he'd ever heard Muscotti discussing who he was and what he did in such an intimate way. It was unnerving in a peculiar way that Balzic couldn't identify; it was almost embarrassing. In another way, Balzic was annoyed to the point of anger. Here was a life-time criminal asking a cop for commiseration because he'd just been humiliated.

Muscotti's eyes came alive suddenly. "I fixed their asses," he said. "I don't own nothin'. I never did have my name on much paper. But now it ain't on no paper. They want ten percent? They can have ten percent of nothin'. You know when I did that? Huh? When I found out they were bringing that scumball Leo Buckles in to open that sex business. I said, hey, maybe they don't care who they work with, but I ain't gonna subsidize that pile of pus."

Balzic scraped his thumbnail across his chin several times. "So are these the people you said her son was with, is that what you're tellin' me?"

"Is this what I'm tellin' ya? Jesus Christ, I just cut my wrist and let my blood run all over you and you're asking me about that lush's kid? Fuck him. This is me I'm talkin' about."

"Well, number one, that's how this conversation got started. You were tryin' to tell me how her kid was in with some heavy hitters. Next thing I know, you're tellin' me all this other stuff about you, and you get this goofy look on your face like I'm supposed to be sympathizing for your, uh, your new position in life, or something, I don't know what."

Muscotti looked positively wounded. "Hey, a little sympathy, that wouldn't be out of line. Especially between friends—"

"Friends!" Balzic snorted. "Who? You and me? Since when have you and me been friends? Jesus Christ. Friends charge friends twenty dollars for a goddamn drink? Where the hell'd you ever get the idea we were anything but what we were? You're the *goombah* and I'm a cop."

"Oh. That's the way it is, huh? Guess I'm dumber than I thought."

"Hey, I don't know what game you're playin', but this wounded friend routine, this is bullshit. If we're such good friends, tell me why I never saw the inside of your house? All those times I drove you home, you ever invite me in? All those Sunday dinners you had for all your *paisans*, what, you have a place set for me and I forget to show up, is that how it was?"

"Hey, those dinners, that was business. Wouldn't look right if you was there. I mean, you couldn't've been there."

"With you, Dom, everything was business. Only now, you don't have any business anymore. So, uh, *now* we're friends. I'm gonna tell you what we were. We had an understanding about certain violations of the *Crimes Code. That* was the game. That was maybe what you thought was friendship, but that was the game. But the game's still on. And, according to you, the understanding you and me had is history. You're history, the understanding's history, but the game ain't. There's a whole new set of rules and a whole new team, and you're such a great friend of mine, you haven't given me one name. You're trying to hustle me on the tab, you're trying to hustle me back here, and we're friends. Right. I'm convinced."

Muscotti tried gamely to put on a soft face. "Hey, you know, old rules, old habits, they're hard to break. C'mon, lemme buy you a drink."

"You don't have to buy me a drink. All you have to do is charge me what you'd charge any civilian who walked in off the street."

"There's customers out here, you know? Huh?"

"Give her a drink," Balzic said, stepping around Muscotti. "I got to make a phone call." He went up to the pay phone on the landing near the rear door and called his home.

"Ruth? It's me. Any word yet?"

"Nothing. I called twice. I got the nursing supervisor both times, and she didn't know anything. You coming home soon?"

"Yeah, pretty soon. I have to take the victim's mother home, that's all, then I'll be home. I was gonna try to talk to her, but she's a juicer. So I won't be too long. She lives up the Terrace. You want me to get anything? Milk, bread?"

"I just want you to come home."

Balzic said he would as soon as he could and hung up. He went back to the bar and finished his beer without talking. Mrs. Blaskevich was rambling; she seemed to be chewing Muscotti out about something. Muscotti was ignoring her and staring off at the front door.

Balzic kicked around whether he should ask Muscotti again for a name, any name, of just one of the heavy hitters he'd said Blaskevich had been doing business with. Balzic thought it was worth a try, so he did.

Muscotti glared at him, "My name's Dominic Muscotti. I'm a bartender. I don't know anything about any heavy hitters. Why don't you and your girlfriend here go home? I'm gettin' ready to close."

Well, Balzic thought, that's what twenty seconds of honesty gets you. You get to slam the door in your own face.

"C'mon, Mrs. Blaskevich, time to go home."

"Don't wanna go home. Wanna drink."

"Yeah, right, I'll bet you do. Here, give me your arm. . . ."

Five minutes later he dropped her into the front seat of his cruiser. He called for another officer to meet him at her address to help get her inside. It took both of them to carry her in, and it was a good thing she'd forgotten to lock the door earlier because she had passed out.

$$* \quad * \quad * \quad * \quad *$$

The next morning, early, the nursing supervisor told Balzic his mother's condition had not changed. She seemed to be resting, she seemed to be in no discomfort, and it would be up to the doctor to reveal the results of any tests that had been made, if, in fact, any had. The supervisor sort of doubted it.

"My god, Mario, what are you doing up? What time did you go to sleep? I didn't hear you come into the bedroom."

"I slept on the couch."

"What did the hospital say? You want some cereal?"

"I had some juice and a cup of coffee. Hospital doesn't know any more now than it did last night. Why don't you go back to sleep? Then you wanna go up the hospital around nine or so? I'll pick you up."

"I'll drive myself. I'll see you there."

Balzic grunted, kissed her on the cheek, and drove to the station. Before he'd closed the outside door to the dutyroom, his shoulders sank. The Rev. P. Shaner Weier was pacing about, fidgeting. He'd obviously been pestering Desk Sergeant Joe Royer, whose lips were pursed tight; he was giving one-word answers to Weier's questions.

"Ah, there. You've arrived. Well," Weier said, "you see what this filth leads to? You see?"

"What filth?" Balzic said, slipping around Weier and through the lift-door in the counter.

"What filth? The—THE filth. Now—not a day after I warned you of the existence of that place—now there's a murder. You see how this escalates? This pictorial degradation of the flesh leads directly to—"

"How'd you find out about that?" Balzic interrupted him.

"On my scanner. I've always been chaplain to the police, every parish I've been called to—"

Balzic interrupted him again: "We don't have a chaplain."

"You don't have a chaplain? Every PD should have a chaplain. I've been trained in crisis counseling. I've also been trained in post-stress syndrome. If you don't have a trained person in these areas, you've got problems, real problems, I can tell you."

Weier tried to lift the door in the counter. Balzic slammed it down. "Unless you're invited in, sir, stay on the other side of the counter."

Balzic turned to Royer and whispered, "How long's he been here?"

"Six o'clock."

"Oh for crissake." Balzic sighed and turned back to face Weier. "Reverend, I can see you're a man with a lotta time on your hands. Let me put you wise right now. I don't want you hangin' around here. I—"

"What do you mean, 'hanging around'? I resent the implication of that—"

"'Hangin' around' means exactly what it says. Bein' here, buttin' in, puttin' your face in our face, mindin' our business. I got no time for law-and-order groupies. I want you to leave and I don't' want you comin' back."

Weier coughed and cleared his throat several times and tried to throw back his shoulders. "I am not a groupie. I am a citizen first, a clergyman second. As such, my observation and knowledge of social events leads me to work with civil authorities. I have always worked with civil authorities, and I shall continue to work with them."

"If you don't get outta here, I'm gonna bust you for harassment. I'm not gonna tell you again: Go away."

"This is preposterous. Yesterday I brought you information about a place blatantly violating the laws of this commonwealth and you refused to even consider prosecution. Now that a murder has been committed on that very property, you're threatening me with arrest for asking you what you're doing about it."

"What you're tryin' to do is get yourself a job as a chaplain for this department, and there is no such job. Yesterday, you were complainin' about porn. Today, you're back because you heard on a scanner about a crime. What I'm tellin' you is, I recognize guys like you. You wanna hang around cops. You're like guys who wanna hang around robbers, or football players, or politicians. I don't know what it is with you guys, but I recognize you when I see you. And I don't allow that. It's a pain in everybody's ass. So good-bye. I'm not jokin'. Get out."

"Excuse me, excuse me," Weier said, coughing and clearing his throat, "but this is a public building. City Hall, in fact. A place where public business is conducted, and I am a citizen, a civilian in this municipality. I have every right granted by law to be here."

"Uh, yesterday you were quotin' the *Crimes Code* at me. You know what the *Code* says about harassment? Huh? Where's a copy of the *Code*? You got one, Joe?"

"Back on the shelf."

"Yeah, right." Balzic went to a bookcase against the rear wall of the dutyroom, retrieved a copy of the *Crimes Code*, and thumbed through it until he found what he was looking for. "Here. 'Section 2709. A person commits a summary offense when, with intent to harass, annoy, or alarm another person: (1) he strikes, shoves, kicks, or otherwise'—never mind that. Here's the part. Paragraph two: 'he follows a person in or about a public place or places: or (3) he engages in a course of conduct or repeatedly commits acts which alarm or seriously annoy such other person and which serve no legitimate purpose.' You hear that? You are seriously annoying me in a public place for no legitimate purpose. You hear that?"

"In whose opinion?"

"In whose opinion what?"

"In whose opinion are my actions a serious annoyance serving no legitimate purpose?"

"Whose do you think? Mine."

"Well," huffed Weier, "you're certainly entitled to your opinion, but in our system of justice your opinion of the law carries no more weight than mine does. So arrest me. And we'll see what a judge and jury has to say."

"A summary offense isn't tried in front of a judge and jury. It's handled by a district justice. Lowest level."

"Well?"

"Well what?"

"Well arrest me. And we'll see how the district justice sees it."

"Why don't you just go away so we can avoid all that? I really got better things to do."

"And that's precisely why I'm here. To see that you do them."

Balzic's chin sank, and he glared over the tops of his glasses at Weier. "I don't need you to tell me how to do anything, don't need you to watch me do anything. What I need is for you to leave. I'm tryin' to make it easy for you to leave, so it can be easy for Sergeant Royer here and for me. You're really hung up on this attachment you have for cops."

"You make it sound perverse. And it is not that way at all."

"It never is to the pervert. Pervert always thinks what he does is what everybody does—or would if they only had the brains or the guts. So naturally you think what you do—what you wanna do—is part of your civic responsibility. But it ain't. Just go take care of the people in your church, why don't you? You mind your business, we'll mind ours, everything'll be fine, okay?"

The phone rang then, Royer answered it, listened for a moment, then motioned for Balzic to pick up a phone.

"Hello, Chief Balzic, what's on your mind?"

"Yeah, Chief, this is Leo Buckles. I just got a call from a state trooper said you want to talk to me. So what's on your mind?"

"Uh-ha. Did that trooper tell you what happened at your porn store last night?"

"Yes, he did."

"Did he also tell you what we wanted you to do?"

"Well, Chief, he said something about talkin' to one of my employees, but I didn't really understand what he wanted me to say to that man."

"Okay. Your employee apparently refuses to say anything to us until he has your approval. So we have a good idea that he saw the person or persons who, uh, committed a crime and we want to know what he knows."

"I see. Well, tell me something. The trooper who called me said something about if I didn't cooperate I was gonna have an unnatural disaster—I think that's the way he said it—d'you know anything about that? 'Cause see, I'm pretty much shocked and disturbed by that kinda talk, if you know what I mean. I mean, policemen talkin' about unnatural disasters, that disturbs me so much I wanna call some friends of mine down in the attorney general's office, see what I mean?"

"I do, yes, I do. I see exactly what you mean. But if your employee doesn't start talkin' to us real soon, you better hope you don't get put on hold by somebody in Harrisburg, 'cause I guarantee you will have an unnatural disaster. Today."

"I see. Well. Perhaps I neglected to tell you something. In fact, I'm sure I forgot. But what I want to tell you is this—this conversation through the magic of modern Japanese technology, has been recorded, and everything you've said is on tape."

"No good, Mr. Buckles. Many, many cases have been decided: A taping is good only if the taper warns the tapee immediately. And you didn't warn me. You worked what, if a cop did it, would be a sort of telephone entrapment. You more or less goaded me into making certain statements and *then* you told me I was on tape. Don't work. You gotta tell me first. Or else you gotta be a cop with a court order, and you ain't. So quit talkin' to me, call your worker, and tell him to be a good citizen, okay? Nice talkin' to you, Mr. Buckles. Good-bye."

Balzic hung up at the same time the Reverend Weier was coming through the lift-door in the counter.

"What in the hell do you think you're doin'?" Balzic said.

"I want to talk to you privately," Weier said.

Balzic looked at Royer, closed his eyes, shook his head, sighed out a breath that puffed his cheeks, and grabbed the Reverend Weier's left hand with his own left, spun Weier around, slid his right arm under Weier's left elbow, and caught hold of Weier's neck with his right hand, and, pulling Weier's left hand down so that he hyperextended Weier's elbow, led him on tiptoes back through the counter. Balzic waited for Royer to get ahead of them to open the outside door, then led Weier, still on tiptoe and making sounds as though someone was depressing his tongue with a flat stick, out onto the steps leading to the parking lot. There, he released him.

Weier's mouth was gaping, and he stabbed the air with his left hand several times, trying to regain feeling in his arm. "What is wrong with you?" he shrieked. "Why do you reject me? Why do you refuse my help? This is what I do—I help the police. It's my ministry!"

Balzic heaved another sigh. "I got thirty-two people in this department plus two meter maids and I can't remember right now how many in the auxiliaries. I guarantee you there's not six Protestants in the bunch. First of all, I don't like your point of view. But that's personal. What ain't personal is that you're tryin' to attach yourself to this department, and this department is mostly Roman Catholic. Some of these people went through twelve years of school with the nuns: They're fuckin' rabid. They see you hangin' around, they're gonna start foamin' at the mouth. And that, Reverend Weier, is a kind of hassle I can live without. I don't want it, I don't need it, and I ain't gonna have it. So take a walk, and don't come back."

"But I can help you," Weier sputtered.

Balzic threw up his hands, clapped them over his ears, and left Weier on the steps.

Balzic hurried back inside and found himself amidst the changing of the watch. He spotted Detective Ruggiero Carlucci and motioned for him to come into his office.

"Mornin', Mario, what's up? Hya doin'? I'm not doing real good myself. I hate this time of the day. I can't believe how many people are up and movin' around already. What's wrong with 'em?"

"They're all nuts, I guess, what do I know? Listen, you still in court—what're you doin' here?"

"I just came in to check my mailbox, that's all. Yeah, I'm still in court. Why?"

"D'you check out that minister I told you to check out?"

"Hey, Mario, you know what it's like in court, you—"

"You didn't check him out, right?"

"No, but—"

"Never mind. Listen to me. I don't care what you're doin', you check this sonofabitch out, you hear?"

Carlucci rolled his eyes. "Hey, Mario, what the hell. I can't be in two places at once. I'm good, Jesus Christ, but I ain't that good."

"When you're sittin' around the witness room, get to a phone and check him out. And don't tell me you can't do it."

"Okay okay okay. Jeez. Where's he from again—New Castle?"

"Right."

"Okay, I'll see what I can do," Carlucci said. "Uh, am I lookin' for anything special?"

"No. I'm not gonna say. Whatever there is, okay?"

"Okay. Oh. Before I forget, my mother said she heard your mother's in the hospital, is that right?"

"Yeah."

"It is? I thought it was some goofy rumor goin' around Norwood. So it's true, huh? What's wrong?"

"The early word is stroke, but I don't know. I haven't seen her since yesterday, last night, and she couldn't talk then. And they were supposed to run all these tests today, I don't know what the hell's goin' on. But thanks for askin'."

"Hey, my mother's coherent for about fifteen minutes every hour, don't ask me how she heard this. I guess from the ladies that sit with her. What am I sayin'—of course. Who else?" Carlucci shrugged feebly. "I hope she's better."

"Me too. Thanks."

"Listen, I'll go call New Castle PD now. I don't have to be in court till ten o'clock. Uh, before I go to court, I'll go light a candle for her, too, okay?"

"Thanks," Balzic said. He turned away so Carlucci wouldn't see the tears that filled his eyes.

* * * * *

Balzic spent the next hour on the phone trying to get somebody at the hospital to tell him how his mother was. None of the nurses would release the results of his mother's tests without the approval of Dr. Bradford James, and James was nowhere to be found. His office secretary kept insisting that he was making rounds in Conemaugh General; the hospital switchboard operator kept insisting that James wasn't answering his page.

In-between calls to James's office and the hospital, Balzic tried to locate Coroner Wallace Grimes, but there was no answer at his office, and he wasn't answering his page either.

Balzic gave up at eight o'clock, told Desk Sergeant Vic Stramsky where he was going, and drove to the hospital. He found Ruth in the waiting room outside the neuro-trauma unit.

"So," he said, dropping into a molded plastic chair beside her, "what's the word?"

"I don't know," Ruth said, closing the book she was reading. "They wheeled her away at about ten after seven and I haven't heard a thing since. They said they were going to do some kind of scan. I don't know whether they said brainscan or CATscan or what. I went after them and every time I asked what they were going to do, this one little . . . twerp, she said I should just go have a seat, they'd take real good care of her. Honest to god, I felt like smackin' her one."

"Well, I been tryin' to call James and his office says he's here and this place says he ain't answerin' his page, so, there we are."

"D'you get anything to eat?"

"Tell you the truth I don't remember. How'd she look? You get to see her before they took her?"

"For about five minutes. She looked just like she looked yesterday."

"She awake?"

"Yeah. Her eyes were open. She looked like she knew who I was. But maybe I just think that 'cause that's what I want to think."

Balzic took off his glasses and peered at the lenses. "Jesus, no wonder I can't see anything. These things are filthy."

"Mario, we have to talk about what we're going to do."

"I thought we already decided about that."

"You were real angry with me when you decided. You were just trying to get me to shut up about it."

"No, I wasn't. I told you the only guy I'd let touch her. You want me to call him up, start makin' arrangements, is that where we're at?"

"You're getting mad again, Mario."

"Goddamn right I'm gettin' mad again. That's my mother I'm talkin' about. I'm talkin' about callin' a fuckin' funeral home . . . Jesus Christ, this is not somethin' I've had a whole lotta experience dealin' with, you know? I'm new at this shit. And I don't like it and I don't like bein' new at it and my brains and my guts are both goin' about eighty in a fifteen-mile-a-hour zone, if that makes any sense."

"Me too, Mario. But other people are not going to do this for us. So that leaves us. And being mad is not going to help, believe me."

"I didn't say I was mad at you."

"I didn't say you did. But when you get mad and there's nobody else around, it sort of makes me think I'm the person you're mad at."

"Jesus Christ, Ruth, sometimes it's just . . . it's just the situation you're mad at. You're just pissed at life for . . . for, shit, for doin' what it does. Doesn't mean I'm pissed at you."

"Well being pissed off doesn't help you and it sure as hell doesn't help me, so I wish you'd figure out some other way to be right now."

"I just can't turn this off, you know? I mean, I didn't purposely turn it on."

"Well, I wish to hell you'd try to turn it off. It's starting to make me mad."

"Okay okay, I get the message." He stood up. "Uh, listen, I'm gonna try to find the coroner. I'll be back as soon as I can, okay?"

"Okay. I'll be here."

"Okay. See ya."

Ruth nodded and gave a little wave. Then she opened her book and resumed reading. He looked back over his shoulder twice on his way to the elevators, but she didn't look up.

* * * * *

Finding Coroner Grimes took only a few minutes. He was in his office. Breaking into the line of people who had business with him took up most of two hours. It seemed to Balzic that every doctor in the hospital and half the lawyers had something to discuss with Grimes that could not wait.

Balzic finally bullied his way into Grimes's office ahead of what appeared to be an entire law firm.

Grimes was sitting stiffly behind his desk, looking distracted.

"I know this is a bad time, Doc," Balzic said, "but I don't think there's gonna be a good time today—Jesus, you look like hell."

"Well, I suppose it's because I've never been able to understand why people think it's my fault when they don't hear what they want to hear. It's probably the only part of this job I've never been able to accept."

"Uh-ha," Balzic said. "Listen. Another time, another place, we could probably have a good time kickin' that around, people's expectations and all that shit, but right now all I wanna know is what else you came up with on the body we found behind the porn store."

"Nothing new, if that's what you mean. Twenty-nine puncture wounds, all made with the same blade, all coming more or less from the same direction: right to left and with exceptional emotion. Six in the genitals. The testicles and scrotum were . . . well, that was an intensity of assault I don't recall seeing before."

"Uh-ha. Uh, you wouldn't want to speculate anymore about who we might be lookin' for, would you?"

"Only if I never have to say this under oath."

"C'mon, Doc."

Grimes shrugged and toyed with a pencil on his desk, turning it end over end. "I think I said last night that there had been a miscalculation made. I've seen nothing to change that assumption. I think the victim was homosexual, that he made the worst misjudgment of character he could have made, and that he is no longer alive because of that."

"What about the character he misjudged?"

"Well, this is probably someone very confused about who he

is, especially sexually, probably someone with a great conflict in his mind about moral behavior. . . ." Grimes took off his glasses and chewed thoughtfully on the stem of one earpiece.

"What kind of conflict?"

"Oh, the usual sort of male conflict we find here in America. Supposed to be strong, silent, tough as nails, and ready for sex all night long and scared to death because he likes his buddies too much and he thinks somebody's taken notice. It's an old story in this country. I don't know why it is, but I do know *that* it is. If I really wanted to fly on the wind of speculation, I'd say that he was probably caught between a very hostile father and a very religious mother. And that's all off the record. On the record, all I'll say with certainty is that the killer of this young male homosexual was a young, right-handed American male, and that the instrument he used was a blade no more than three-quarters of an inch wide and no more than three and one-half inches long. All the rest of my speculation is just that and nothing more—not very scientific, more in the realm of psychopathology, for which I am totally unqualified."

Balzic nodded several times and stared at Grimes. "You know, I've known you for twenty-some years—I forget how many exactly—and this is the longest I've ever heard you talk at one time. You okay?"

"No. Not really. I've just spent most of my time today telling people facts they did not want to be told and most of them seemed to take it personally and seemed, furthermore, to think that if they just had the chance to do some shopping—pathologically speaking—they could find the bargains they're after. Most of the time I have no trouble with that. Most of the time I'm able to say very easily, 'Well if you want to take the raw data to another pathologist, go right ahead. It's not going to change.' Today, I just had too much of lawyers lawyering and relatives trying to find somebody to blame for death. And when you tell them there isn't anyone to blame—it just happened—why you'd think it was my fault that I couldn't find a fault. As I said, most of the time I have no problem with this. Most of the time, it's part of the job description: must contend with irrational, illogical responses to the declaration of rational, logical, scientific fact. Just got to me today, that's all. Anything else,

Mario? I've got a thumping headache all of a sudden and I don't have one aspirin in this place. I've got to go down the trauma unit."

"No, nothing else. Just a copy of the report, huh? Couple days? Right?"

"Don't expect it before then. I'm way behind."

Balzic shrugged as though to say that was fine with him, he'd take whatever he could get. He shouldered his way through the law firm he'd bullied past on his way in to see Grimes. There were four of them—the oldest in his sixties, the youngest in his twenties—and they had about them a predatory brightness, a sparkly kind of hunger that nearly made Balzic shiver. He could imagine them jogging together, working out together, planning their case strategies and tactics, after which they'd sit around comparing pulse-recovery times and levels of low- and high-density lipoproteins and the up-to-the-absolute-latest-minute research on which color necktie gave the most power.

Balzic wouldn't have known anything about power ties if it hadn't been for Mo Valcanas. About two weeks before, Valcanas had regaled him for nearly an hour one night with his power-tie index. Valcanas said he began every day in court with a stroll through the halls, counting red neckties. "One day," Valcanas had said, "every goddamn tipstaff I saw had a red tie on, even Nate Verdugo. So I asked Nate how much clout he had and he got all googly-eyes and said he thought he had some in World War II when he made corporal but he was pretty sure he didn't have any now. He couldn't even get his daughter a job in the courthouse custodial department."

Every one of those four lawyers had a red tie on. Balzic silently wished Grimes well and set off down the hall toward the neuro-trauma unit, hoping that his mother had been brought back from whatever scan she's had and he could talk to her.

He found Ruth in the same chair, still reading.

"Not back yet, huh?"

"Oh, she's been back and gone again. Some kind of mixup or scheduling."

"How'd she look? You get to talk to her?"

"The same. No, I didn't talk to her. Just when the nurses got her settled in her bed, not thirty seconds after they walked out,

67

here came two other nurses to cart her off again. She just looked bewildered, that's all. I didn't get to say anything to her. Look, I'm getting hungry. I think I'm going to go to the cafeteria. You want to do that or not?"

"No. Think I'll go down to Muscotti's. I could use a beer. She got a phone? Is it hooked up yet?"

"Nobody's said a word to me about it."

"Well why don't you get it hooked up and I'll call you. I don't know where the hell I'm gonna be, okay?"

"All right," she said. "Mario, try to slow down a little. There's nothing you can do to make anything go faster. Remember? We're at the mercy of strangers. You've told me that more times than I can remember. We've got to have faith they know what they're doin', that's what you've always told me."

"Yeah? Well that's just another one of my sunshine enemas." He studied the floor for a moment. "I'm goin' to Muscotti's. Don't wear yourself out here, okay? Take a break every once in a while, go home, go for a walk, okay?"

"I'll be okay."

"Okay. So I'll see you later."

Balzic walked Ruth to the cafeteria and left her there, promising to call as soon as he'd finished lunch and checked out his station. He walked to Muscotti's. It was a dreary day, clammy and cloudy. When he got inside Muscotti's he found the mood as sour as the weather.

"Don't tell me I didn't turn in your goddamn number," Vinnie the bartender was saying to his brother Jimmy the barber. "I don't forget shit like that."

"Then how come nobody's paying me off?"

"'Cause you didn't play the goddamn number, that's how come."

"I stood right here Friday and told you two-thirty-six box on the old stock."

"You weren't even in here on Friday for crissake, so how'd you play anything? Huh?" Vinnie came down the bar to where Balzic had found an empty stool. "Whatta you gonna have?"

"Whatta you got to eat?"

"I got roast beef on a hill, hollowed out. You want one?"
Balzic nodded.

"What to drink?"

"Beer."

"Why do you do this to me, Vince?"

"Why do you do this to me, Jimmy? Huh? You try this shit, same old shit, every two, three years. It ain't never worked before, it ain't working now, it ain't never gonna work. You come in here and embarrass me in front of all my friends and customers."

"What do you think you do to me when you tell me I didn't play the number I played with you?"

"How many fuckin' times I gotta tell you I don't book no numbers, huh? I been tellin' you for thirty-fuckin'-five years I don't book no numbers. All the fuck I am is a goddamn announcer. The books come in, they say what's up, and I give 'em the news. All I am is like one of them guys with hairspray on TV, that's all."

"Don't curse like that no more. Ma would have a heart attack she heard you talking to me like that."

"Oh yeah, right," Vinnie growled, "get 'em all outta the cemetery. Line 'em up. Get 'em in the lockerroom, get 'em into uniforms, get 'em out of the field. Jimmy's Dream Team, Ma, Pa, and Uncle Louie, here they come, they're all suited up, they're all gettin' ready to blitz. I'm backed up on the two-yard line, first and ten, and Jimmy's gonna blitz me with the whole family." Vinnie disappeared into the kitchen. In about two minutes, he was back, sliding a plate with a roast-beef sandwich on it in front of Balzic.

"Hey, Mario, you gotta pay for this," Vinnie whispered, leaning over the bar.

"Huh? Why?"

Vinnie shrugged. "First thing I found when I come in this morning was a note from Dom. Said, 'No tab for Mario. He's shut off.' And don't start with me, okay? I got enough with my brother here, I don't need no more from nobody, okay?"

Balzic held up his hands and nodded. "How much?"

"Three bucks and we're straight."

"That's how much I give you," Jimmy said. "Three bucks. I should be collecting fifteen seventy-five today at least." He shook his head and stomped toward the front door.

"Giddoutta here. Go cut some more heads. Don't bother me no more about this shit. You never bet three bucks on nothin' in your life."

"Some day I hope you don't have to answer for this," Jimmy said at the door.

"Yeah, right. That's what I hope, too."

Jimmy gritted his teeth so hard his head and neck quivered. Then he was gone.

"Sometimes," Vinnie said sadly, shaking his head and speaking to no one in particular, "sometimes I think my brother's gonna get as nuts as my Uncle Louie, and he was the nuttiest fuck that ever was."

He stared at Balzic. "I ever tell you what my Uncle Louie did one time? Huh?"

"No. I mean, what one time are you talkin' about?"

"One time my Uncle Louie, he only had two suit coats and a topcoat, so he takes a razor blade and cuts the lining out of all those coats. My Aunt Philly, she goes nuts. She asks him what the hell he thinks he's doin'. He says he's lookin' for the money. 'What money?' she says. 'The money I sewed in there before I come to this country,' he says. 'Well, where is it?' she says. And he says, 'I don't know. It ain't there no more. Somebody must've took it.' So help me, that's what he said, 'Somebody must've took it. It ain't there no more.' I was a little kid when he said that. And now my brother's starting to get like Louie. Jesus, I don't believe it."

"What's wrong with Jimmy? Something wrong with him?"

"What the fuck do I know? I tried to talk him into goin' to the VA hospital down in Oakland. He said he don't need to go. I tell him, 'Hey, Jimmy, you're losin' it. Maybe it was them fuckin' howitzers you were listenin' to the whole war.' He tells me get lost. You know, without hearing aids, Jimmy's practically deaf. It's from the fuckin' artillery. And I swear, last coupla years, I think he's hearin' things inside. Like he's pickin' up call-in shows on his fillings or somethin'."

"Hey, you can't help him if he doesn't want it. If he's no danger to himself or to other people, you're not gonna get a psychiatric evaluation. I don't know what the federal policy is, you know, with the VA, but I do know you can't do anything

70

with the county unless there's a threat of physical danger. Besides, he's got a wife and kid."

Vinnie shook his head. "He married a puppy. She don't do nothin' 'less he tells her. And his kid's gone."

"Whatta you mean gone?"

"Gone gone. He went to Canada to get outta Vietnam. He's still there."

"Didn't he ever hear about the amnesty?"

"I don't know what he heard. All I know is I get a Christmas card from Toronto every year. But he ain't coming back for nothin'. He won't come back for their funerals, I know he won't. He's a stubborn fucker."

Balzic shrugged. "Sounds to me like it's outta your hands."

"I know it is," Vinnie said, "but he's my brother, you know? I can't just let him wander around runnin' his mouth. I mean, it ain't as though he's doin' that all the time, you know what I'm sayin'? But at the same time, I don't want him hurtin' himself either."

"Has he hurt himself yet?"

"Huh? No. No, not yet."

"Then I'd assume he wasn't goin' to. And I'd keep on assumin' that until he did otherwise. And then I'd go from there. And I know you didn't ask for my advice."

"I understand. But I appreciate what you're tellin' me. Oh-oh. Hide the silver. Here comes the long arm of the Pope."

"Good afternoon to you too," said Father Marrazo, hustling in and hiking himself up on a stool next to Balzic.

"Hey, Father, what's up? Hy ya doin'?"

"Mario, how are you? Vince, just coffee, okay? Please?"

"You look like a man on a mission," Balzic said after swallowing his last bite of sandwich and wiping his mouth.

"I am," the priest said guardedly. "Why don't we go sit at a table—near the wall. Please?"

"Hey, sure. Of course. I was just kiddin'—I see you're not."

They waited until Vinnie had brought coffee for the priest and refilled Balzic's glass with draft beer, then they went to a table against the far wall.

"So, Father, what's up?"

"I just had a very disturbing conversation on the phone with a woman who wouldn't tell me who she was. She said she thinks her son's in trouble, she thinks he's done something 'real bad.' But no matter how I pumped her, she wouldn't tell me what she thought he'd done."

"Can't even make a guess who she is?"

The priest shrugged.

"She has to be from the parish, right? Why would she call you if she wasn't?"

"Can't imagine."

"Well," Balzic said, sipping his beer, "how many mommas you know have bad boys?"

"You're not taking this very seriously."

"Well you just said yourself she wouldn't tell you what she thought he'd done no matter how you pumped her. So what am I supposed to do? Interview every momma in the parish who thinks her son's done somethin' real bad? How long you think that'd take?"

The priest stirred his coffee absently and fixed his gaze on some point over Balzic's shoulder.

"Uh, Father, what's the problem here? You know? Or don't you know?"

"I guess I don't know," the priest said, his gaze focusing once again on Balzic.

Balzic pursed his lips and sighed. "Uh, don't take this wrong, Father, okay? But either you lost some of the high cards in your deck or else you're not tellin' me somethin'."

The priest coughed and cleared his throat. "What's happened—bad, I mean?"

"Well, World War II wasn't real great, C'mon, Father, what're you talkin' about here? Bad, when? When—1950, last week, last night?"

The priest's shoulders rose and fell as he took several deep breaths. "She found a lot of blood."

"Uh-ha. So? She tell you this in confession?"

"No."

"Well if she didn't tell you in confession, what's the problem?"

"The problem is she didn't identify herself. She wanted my counsel. What do I tell her?"

"What did you tell her?"

"I told her to tell him to call the police."

Balzic splayed his hands. "So? You told her right."

"Mario, was anyone killed recently? Murdered?"

"Don't know if it was murder. But somebody was sure killed."

"When?"

"Last night."

"Was it bloody?"

"Definitely."

"Oh my."

"'Oh my' what?"

"She said her son drinks a lot, she said she woke him up this morning 'cause she found him asleep on the couch on the back porch, covered with a rug and when he stood up and the rug fell off him, that's when she saw all the blood. They both thought there was something wrong with him, because there was so much blood and it was all over him, they thought maybe he'd been in an accident. So he took all his clothes off and didn't find anything wrong. In the bathroom, I mean he did that. He didn't take his clothes off in front of his mother."

"She said she took his word for it? She didn't actually see for herself that he was okay, there was nothing wrong with him?"

"Would that make a difference?"

Balzic shrugged. "Lots of goofy people around, Father, you know that as well as I do. Some of 'em bloody other people . . . hey, you know what I'm talkin' about."

The priest looked puzzled, shook his head, and after a moment said, "Well what are we going to do?"

"Well, unless you can think of a family with a religious mother, a violent father, and a confused son, or unless that woman calls you back and gives you a name and address, we can't do anything about it."

"Religious mother, violent father, confused son—did I miss something here?"

"That's a profile, I guess you'd call it, the coroner gave me. Says the killing was done by the confused son. And here you are tellin' me about a phone call you got from a mother. So that part fits." Balzic eyed the priest with a greater intensity. "You have told me everything, right? You're not leavin' anything out?"

"Why do I suddenly feel accused?" Marrazo said, laughing.

"I give up. Why do you?" Balzic said, also laughing. "It's a joke, Father. Forget it."

"I wonder."

"Nah, nah. For sure, it's a joke. Honest."

"Listen, Mario, if I knew who the woman was, I would tell you, believe me."

"C'mon, Father. I know that. I'm tellin' you, it was a joke."

"Okay," the priest said warily. "If you say so."

"I do. Really. So, anything she said stick out in your mind?"

"Like what?"

"Like anything, a different way of talkin', a different word, a different phrase, a different tone of voice, anything that reminds you of anybody you know."

The priest thought for a long moment. "No. Nothing distinctive."

"Well, if she calls back and she still doesn't give her name, pay attention to the way she talks. And tell her to call me. Not just the police. That's too impersonal for some people. Give her my name, tell her I'm one of the good guys, tell her I won't hurt her kid, tell her all the nice-nice crap. Pump a little sunshine up her dupa."

The priest nodded. "Can I get you another beer?"

"Nah. I gotta go back up the hospital. My mother's . . . she's not doin' too good."

"Oh, Mario, I'm sorry. Can I do anything? Please let me help. What's wrong?"

Balzic shrugged. "Early word is she's had at least one stroke. But that was last night. Today we can't get any words. Startin' to piss me off. Listen, if I need your help, believe me, I'll call you. And maybe you . . . maybe you need to see her." Balzic's voice cracked.

"Oh, Mario, absolutely. I have to go there anyway to see Sam Ferrante and his wife."

"What's wrong with them?"

"Oh, it's terrible. Everything went wrong with him. He's got bowel problems, kidney, heart, and she's had a heart attack. They've been married for sixty years and he's never been sick. And the only time they were apart was during the war. From what I heard, she collapsed after they got him in bed and told her she had to leave the room for a couple of minutes. She went out in the hall and boom, down she went."

"That's a shame. He's a nice guy. So's she. Nice lady. Well listen, if you're gonna see them, please stop and see my mother. And if you can't see her, at least talk to Ruth, okay?"

The priest stood to go, searching through his pockets for money to pay for his coffee.

"That's okay, Father, I got it."

"No no no, that's not the point. I'm starting to forget things. Not only don't I have any money, now I can't find my keys."

"Maybe you left 'em in the car."

"I walked."

Balzic shrugged. "Two weeks ago, my mother was talkin' to me about somethin', she stopped and she looked at me and I asked her what's the matter, and she says she can't remember my name. I thought she was jokin', but her eyes filled up and she came and put her hand on my face, you know. And I told her what my name was, I said, 'I'm Mario.' And she just kind of, I don't know, drifted off. When, uh, when your memory doesn't work, boy it shakes your ass. It really does. So, listen, you gettin' any complaints about the porn store?"

"About the what?"

"I guess not. Never mind. On the other hand, you get any complaints about the porn store, let me know, will you?"

"Sure. Of course. Will you . . ." The priest nodded toward the empty cup.

"I told you I would, don't worry about it."

The priest thanked him and hurried out. Balzic took the cup and saucer and his empty glass to the bar, where Vinnie asked if he wanted a refill.

"Why certainly the man wants a refill. Everybody wants a refill," Panagios Valcanas said, clapping Balzic on the back. "And it's all on an insurance company which shall remain nameless but which was, this very morning, rebuked by the great and learned judges of the state Superior Court for filing a—and I quote—a 'frivolous' appeal. Which means, me mighty buckos, the goddamn check better be in the hands of a reliable messenger by tomorrow or I'm going to raise hell, both holy and unholy. Make mine a double of your finest unwatered gin, if you please, and water back."

"Jesus," Balzic said, "this must've been a beauty."

"Beauty? Truth is beauty and beauty truth and even beauty gets boring if you don't have a little ugliness for comparison. You want beauty? Try seven hundred and fifty thousand beauties—five hundred thousand punitive, two hundred and fifty thou damages. And all I get is forty percent and you know what? I'm feeling so good, I'm going to take twenty-five. That's how goddamn good I feel. What's twenty-five percent of seven hundred fifty big ones, hmmm?"

"One-eighty-seven and a half," piped up Vinnie.

"One-eighty-seven and a half," Valcanas said. "I ask you, have you heard more beautiful words? That leaves my client—"

"Five-sixty-two and a half," said Vinnie.

"The man ought to be workin' for the auditor general, for crissake," Valcanas said.

"Yeah, yeah," Vinnie said. "So am I gonna get paid for all the work I'm doin' today—am I gonna get paid today or am I gonna have to wait till you get your check which is in your mail?"

"Faithlessness is so unbecoming, Vincent, I hardly know how to respond." Valcanas drew his wallet and laid out three twenties on the bar. "I'm staying till that is gone, Vincent, and if I see you cheating me once, you faithless Sicilian, I'm going to smash your fingers with an ashtray. In the meantime, in lieu of a kiss to demonstrate your affection for me, how 'bout fillin' some goddamn glasses, whatta ya say?"

"You know one of the reasons I don't wanna die?" Vinnie asked Balzic.

"No. Why?"

"'Cause I know me and him's goin' to the same place and that means I'm gonna have to listen to this prick forever."

"You're going to live forever?" Valcanas hooted. "You don't know how to occupy yourself for a Sunday afternoon if the TV goes off. Without electricity, you'd have to try to make intelligent conversation, and in your case, that's a contradiction in terms."

Valcanas turned to Balzic. "I can see me now. I'm on the patio by a white-washed house on an island in the Aegean Sea. The sun is almost blinding. I have many bottles of retsina cooling. I am sipping ouzo and coffee at a table under an awning. I am the color of pecans. There's a plate of feta and Kalamata olives and bread. Not that white artificial sponge they call bread here, but real bread. And on a little grill, scallops brushed with sesame oil and lemon juice . . . sweet Jesus, I can smell them now. And grapes. White seedless grapes, a platter heaping with them. And young women, several of them, following me everywhere I go, calling out after me, 'Panagios . . . Panagios.' A hundred and eighty-seven-thousand five-hundred goddamn Yankee dollars, Mario. Mario! Think of it! I could rent a house there on some of those islands for a hundred dollars a month. A bed, a woodstove, a chair, a table, a chamberpot. . . ." Valcanas sighed dreamily, and he tossed back half his glass of gin. Soon all the other patrons were hoisting their glasses to him and his good fortune and hard work, and he was dancing—small, hesitant steps at first—and then he began to sing, some simple song in Greek.

Balzic hated to leave, but he had to.

"Mario," Valcanas was saying as Balzic headed for the door, "we could all go . . . we could drink and dance and eat real bread and real olives. . . . Again, Vincent! Again. . . ."

"Yeah, Balzic said to himself. If only it was that easy.

*   *   *   *   *

Five steps into the main lobby of the hospital, Balzic heard himself being paged. He veered off to the receptionist's desk.

"Where's that page coming from? Where do I take the call?"

The receptionist, a roundish woman with snowy hair, pointed to a phone on the wall near the elevators.

Balzic picked up the phone and identified himself.

"It's me, Mario. Marrazo. She called again. She wants to talk to you."

"The woman with the bloody son?"

"Yes."

"So? Who is she? Where's she live?"

"She wouldn't say—"

"Well how the hell am I supposed—"

"Just a second, wait a second. Let me finish."

"Okay. Go 'head, finish."

"She's coming here. She wants you to park in the back, behind the rectory. She said she'll wait till you get out of your car, then she'll approach you."

"When's this supposed to happen?"

"As soon as you can get here apparently."

"Okay. But first I'm gonna talk to Ruth, see how my mother's doin'. I thought you were comin' up here."

"I intended to, Mario, but the phone was ringing when I came in to get my keys."

"Okay. Hey, do me a favor. Don't take any confessions for a while, okay?"

"Mario, I am not an arm of the state. We've discussed this several times, and I am not going to discuss it now. If someone wants to confess and I am here and I have time—"

"Okay okay okay. So, uh, I'll get there as soon as I can."

Balzic hung up and hustled off to find Ruth. When he did, he learned that she had talked for nearly ten minutes with Dr. James, that his initial diagnosis of a major CVA had been confirmed by blood tests and brainscan and that he was waiting for the result of a test on spinal fluid. Ruth said James was neither more nor less pessimistic than he'd been last night. She finally told Balzic that his mother was dozing and waking and that she seemed to be in no great discomfort.

When Balzic went in to see his mother her eyes were closed. Her breathing seemed normal to him. He was surprised to see only an IV in the back of her hand, and no tubes going into her nose or throat. Not that he would have known what the presence of those technological intrusions would have meant— he was vaguely satisfied to see that the only tube going into her was the IV in the back of her left hand. Her hand looked so frail, her skin so papery, her knuckles so bony. He put his hand on hers and rubbed it with his thumb. He spoke to her twice, but she didn't respond.

He shrugged at Ruth, sighed, and said, "I gotta go talk to a lady. I'll be back as soon as I can. Why don't you go home for a while?"

"I'm not going to do anything at home that I can't do here, so what's the difference? When I get tired, I'll go, don't worry."

"Okay." He kissed her on the cheek and then on the lips and patted her shoulder.

About six minutes later, he was standing beside his cruiser in the parking lot behind Saint Malachy's rectory.

There were at least a half-dozen cars in the lot. Presumably, they belonged to parish employees. No one was in any of them. No one else was in the lot either. What had Marrazo said? "She'll wait until you get out of your car and then she'll approach you"—is that what he'd said?

Balzic leaned his rump against the rear fender of his cruiser and flicked his lower teeth with his thumbnail. "Okay, lady, anytime now'll be fine with me."

Five minutes later, Balzic was beginning to feel more than a little foolish. He'd just lurched forward off the fender, intending to go into the rectory, when he saw a woman coming from the alley that ran past the far end of the parking lot.

She was plain, of medium height, wearing dark clothes, a black raincoat over a charcoal-gray skirt, with dark stockings and black flat shoes. She walked very stiffly, her arms barely moving, her shoulders rounded forward. She had a grayish scarf tied around her hair, and she wore no makeup.

Balzic took a step away from his cruiser and watched her. When she was about fifteen feet or so away from him, she stopped. She looked wooden with fear.

"Are you the police? The policeman? The chief?" Her voice kept cracking with emotion.

"Yes, ma'am. I'm Chief Balzic, Rocksburg Police Department. Father Marrazo says you want to talk to me, is that right?"

"I don't know. I thought I did. But I'm not so sure now." She looked all around the lot.

"Do you want to sit in my car? Do you want to go inside? Or do you want to stay here? Whatever you think'll make you comfortable, we'll do."

She shook her head no many times. "I'm not going to be comfortable anywhere."

"Then let's just stay right here for the time being. Does that suit you?"

"I don't know. I guess."

"Do you wanna tell me your name, ma'am?"

"No."

"Okay. Do you wanna tell me what's on your mind?"

"I want . . . I want to know some things about the law."

"Okay. What things?"

"I know that there are different kinds of . . . ," she swallowed several times and her eyes filled up. She shivered reflexively. "When a person does something, there are different circumstances . . . aren't there?"

"Different degrees, ma'am? Or do you mean mitigating and aggravating circumstances?"

"Yes. All of those . . . things."

"Yes, ma'am, there are those things. Would you like me to give you some examples?"

"Oh. Yes. Yes, I would."

"Well, ma'am, if I hurt somebody because I planned to hurt that person because I wanted revenge against that person or because I would profit from that person's injury, that would be much more serious than if I hurt that person because that person attacked me. Or because I thought the person was going to attack me."

"That's what I thought," the woman said, letting out a very small sigh.

"We're talking about your son, is that right, ma'am?"

"I didn't say that."

"No, you didn't, ma'am, but Father Marrazo did."

"He did?"

"Yes, he did."

"Oh. He didn't tell me he was going to do that."

"Well, he was in pretty much of a corner, ma'am. He wants to help, he's not sure how to do that, he wants to be able to tell you the right thing, so he had to tell me as much as he thought I could handle in order to tell you something he could tell you. That's pretty much the way it went. He wasn't being deceitful with you, he wasn't betraying your confidence."

"Well, he just didn't tell me he was going to tell you that, that's all."

"Well, ma'am, the point is not what *he* did or didn't tell me. The point is what *you* want to tell me, you understand?"

"Well I'm not sure I want to tell you anything. Do *you* understand?"

"Absolutely, ma'am, absolutely. What we're talkin' about now is very general stuff. You agree with that?"

She nodded once, then twice more. She had not changed her position or posture. She seemed to move nothing but her mouth when she talked. Balzic, for his part, kept showing both palms of his hands, as though to say, I'm here, I'm open, I got nothing up either sleeve.

"Yes," she said. "So far that's all we've talked about."

"Well, whatever questions you have, ma'am, if I can answer them, I'll do my best."

She thought for a long moment. "If a person . . . hurt somebody in an accident . . . and he ran away, what would that be?"

"An accident? You mean like a traffic accident? A hit and run, is that what you mean?"

"No. Well, sort of."

Some hit and run that was, Balzic thought. Twenty-nine puncture wounds. "Well, yes, ma'am, our society looks, uh, looks unfavorably on people who deny their responsibility." Jesus Christ, Balzic thought, I keep this up, I'm gonna be sick. I'm startin' to sound like a fuckin' government training film. "Listen, lady, why don't we go inside and sit down with Father Marrazo and maybe you'll feel a little more comfortable."

She backed away two steps abruptly. "No. I don't want to do that."

Balzic held up his hands. "Okay, okay, it was just a suggestion. I thought maybe—but, hey, forget about it. We'll stay right here."

"No. I can't. I have to go." She spun so awkwardly that she nearly fell. Then she bolted stiffly away.

Balzic chased after her until he reached the alley, then he thought that to run after her would be foolish. She'd be back. She was tighter up than the most uptight person he'd ever seen, and he couldn't remember who that was. But he had no doubt that she'd be back. If she didn't tell somebody soon what was going on in her life, she'd snap. This woman might have heard the word *flexible*, but she didn't know what it meant. She couldn't have made a wild guess.

He turned and walked slowly back to his cruiser. He looked up at the back door of the rectory. Father Marrazo was holding it open and waving for him to come in.

Inside, he said, "Were you watchin'?"

The priest nodded.

"So? Who is she?"

"I don't know."

Balzic stiffened, baffled. "What the hell d'you mean, you don't know? D'you get a good look at her?"

"I got a very good look at her. I watched her almost the whole time you were talking with her. I've never seen her before. She's not from this parish."

"Then why the hell'd she call you?"

"You're asking me?" the priest said, as perplexed and frustrated as Balzic.

"Man, I thought she calls you . . . sonofabitch. That would've been too easy. Right now, I would really like for things to be too easy, you know?"

"Well what did she say?"

"Not a whole lot. I can't remember the last time I saw anybody that uptight. I kept lookin' at her face, I was sayin', this woman has eyes, a nose, mouth, eyebrows, hair, cheeks—she's got everything a face is supposed to have, and I'm tellin' you, I was lookin' right at her and I couldn't have described her while I was lookin' at her. She was standin' right in front of me and it was like she was gonna fade right out. I felt so goddamned sorry for her."

"You felt sorry for her? Not just because of her situation?"

"No. I was just thinking of her. I've seen that look so many times I can't tell you how many. It's like somebody's been beatin' the piss outta 'em for so long the only thing they're thinkin' about is findin' a place to hide. And they know they can't hide. They're gonna get found and they're gonna get whipped again and they know there's not a goddamn thing they can do about it. You got any wine?"

"Of course. Let's go back to my office." Marrazo led the way.

Once they'd made their way back to his office, he went to the small refrigerator near his desk and found a bottle of chardonnay. Balzic slumped into a leather wing-back chair.

The priest poured two glasses nearly full and handed one to Balzic. They drank in silence for some moments.

"You think it's her son, don't you?"

Balzic shrugged. "Hey, for all I know, her son might be involved in something I don't know the first thing about. She might be some goofy coincidence. She might not even have a son. She might be an all-state head case. She might think she has a son who keeps turnin' up covered with blood in her hallucinations. Nothing she said had anything to do with the body we found last night."

"You don't believe that."

"Believe it? We talkin' about belief now? If that's what we're talkin' about, Father, what I believe is we got an actor in the White House, and he's got a missus who thinks all you gotta do to get rid of drugs is just say no. What I believe is, the next time I get called out to deal with some biker who's been smokin' PCP and drinkin' beer and poppin' meth for about three days and three nights and is freaked out of his mind—what I believe is I should just sidle on up to him and say, 'Ya know, you oughta just say no to drugs.' And what I believe is, the first missus oughta be standin' right next to me when I say it so she can observe him tryin' to decide how he wants to tear my throat out."

"That's all buzzword politics, Mario, and you know it."

"Of course I know it. You just asked me about my beliefs and I just gave you one. Had nothin' to do with that woman or her son—if she has a son and if he did anything." Balzic held his wine up to the light and stared at it. "What is this?"

"It's from Argentina. Somebody gave it to me, I don't remember who. Supposedly less than five dollars a bottle."

"Doesn't taste like anything I know."

"Somebody said it reminded them of a decent white Bordeaux."

"You think? It doesn't have that real flinty taste those have. I don't know, I like it. I think this could stand up to a real good marinara, whatta you think?"

"Speaking of which, do you know the Lamendolas?"

"Which ones? Dickie or the old man, Paulie?"

"Paulie died last week, Mario."

"Did he really? Jesus, how'd I miss that? What happened? Jeez, I talked to him about two weeks ago, he was fine. He gave me a big bag of red peppers. I fried a whole bunch of 'em in olive oil and garlic, made a sandwich—jeeze, he died. What happened?"

"I don't know. Apparently, his heart. I thought you knew. But anyway, after the funeral, I went to his home. His wife invited us. Mario, I have to tell you, I ate the best marinara sauce I've ever eaten. She told me that was the only way she could get through the night. She must have made five gallons. This huge pot, she was up all night, peeling tomatoes and chopping onions and carrots and garlic, all from their garden."

"Oh, Paulie had the touch. He had the holy hands. One day, I don't know, maybe ten years ago, longer probably, I was cruisin' past his house and he's out on the sidewalk, hollerin' about somethin'. He sees me, waves, hollers, ho, ho, c'mere. So I stop. He takes me in the kitchen, he just came from the State Store, he's got three jugs of red wine in the refrigerator, he's got this huge bowl of stuff on the table, he tells me to sit down, sit down, pours me a water glass full of wine, and gets out an iron skillet and some olive oil and starts makin' these pancakes. And as fast as he's makin' 'em, we're eatin' 'em. And we're drinkin' and he's bitchin' about somebody. I forget who he was pissed off about, his neighbor's wife or somebody, but we ate and drank, I called my wife, told her to bring my mother, we ate and drank until we couldn't move, none of us.

"So finally I said, 'Hey, what are we eatin'?' And he showed me. Zucchini pancakes. He had bushels full of zucchini. And he put 'em through the big holes in a grater, mixed it with a little flour, some olive oil, couple eggs, and then he dropped the batter in the hot olive oil. Couple minutes on each side, turned 'em once, man, I can still taste 'em. I don't know what the hell we talked about, but it was a day I'll never forget. Right after my wife and my mother got there, his wife came home, and his wife and my mother were from, like three miles apart in Italy.

So they were chewin' on some real heavy memories there . . . Jeez, he died. How old was he?"

"Ninety, she said," the priest said, looking off. "I imagine we'll be burying her very soon. She told me that she wished they could've both been hit by a car. She said it was so quiet in the house it hurt her teeth. I asked her what she meant, she said she couldn't help it, she was so mad that he died without her, she kept biting down, and her teeth were all sore."

"Yeah, I've been that mad lotsa times. You just start chompin' down, after a while you got this pain in your mouth, you wonder where it came from. All you have to do is think about it for a couple minutes and you know. Then what I do is—really smart—I get mad at myself for gettin' that mad. It's stupid."

The priest stood and refilled their glasses. When he resumed his seat, they stared at each other. "What were we talking about?"

"Paulie Lamendola. And my mother. And his wife. And her teeth hurtin'. I leave anything out?"

"No. That covers it. But I do think we ought to try to do something about our mood. We get any lower we're going to have to send for psychiatric help."

"Wouldn't do me any good. 'Cause after I got analyzed, I'd have to say that nothing had changed: My mother was still very sick, maybe close to death, and there isn't a goddamn thing I can do about it, and I refuse to accept that. My mind, such as it is, refuses to accept that reality. So what good would it do to talk to a shrink?"

"Might clear up some things," the priest said.

"There's nothin' to clear up. My mother's old, she just had a stroke, she's gonna die, and I'm scared as hell. My mother's smart, tough, funny as hell sometimes, and she never let anybody mess with me when I was a kid. She also never let me get away with anything when I was a kid, or now. Never. My mother never went to school a day in this country. I don't know how far she got in school in Italy. But she taught herself English, she taught herself to read and write. She wasn't any professor, but she could write. She read the paper every day, especially the ads, the personals, lost and found, and articles for sale. She always wanted to know who lost something or found something or what people were sellin'. One day she told me about an ad she read, said it was real sad, somebody was sellin' a wedding gown, never used, and an engagement ring, slightly used.

"But the ads that used to really break her up were the ones that went, 'I, John Smith, am no longer responsible for the debts of my ex-wife, Mrs. John Smith.' Every time my mother read one of those ads, she used to crack up. I'd say to her, 'Hey, Ma, this is just as sad as the wedding gown never used, you know?' And she'd say, 'Oh no, oh no. This is not sad. The guy who put this ad in the paper, he ain't sad, he's so mad he's goin' crazy.' And then she'd start laughin' like hell. I still don't understand why she thought that was so funny. 'Course, she also used to laugh at me when I got mad about somethin' she thought was pretty silly."

They fell silent and sipped their wine, staring at their own memories.

After several minutes had passed, Father Marrazo said, "What are you going to do now?"

Balzic shrugged. "I was kinda hoping I could just stay here for the next two or three years."

"Years? My God."

"Hey, what's wrong with hope? Wasn't for fear, hope wouldn't exist, and I never knew anybody yet who wasn't afraid of somethin'. My biggest fear just happens to be that my mother's gonna die, and I can't even get myself together enough to go sit with her. Scared as hell she's goin', and I can't be with her till she goes. I go into her room, I look at her, I touch her, I get this goddamn tornado in my gut, my head starts ringin', I can't even open my mouth to talk to her. . . ."

"Some of us are good at consolation, some of us aren't," Father Marrazo said. "Look at Reagan. He's a master consoler. Never misses an opportunity to embrace a next of kin. Never misses a funeral or a service where grief is the primary emotion. How do you think he got around that Bitburg thing, that visit to a cemetery where Nazis were buried? He's a wizard at manipulating that kind of emotion. About the only thing he didn't say was, Well, shucks, Nazis have mothers, too, and their mothers miss them and their mothers love them no matter what they did. I'm telling you, Mario, every priest ought to study that man to learn how to turn grief to good advantage."

"Turn grief to what? Good advantage? You kiddin' me or what?"

"Mario, of course I'm not kidding you. Listen, we spend years in seminary studying theology, philosophy, Latin, Greek, and we come out and discover that no amount of Latin or Greek or New Testament text-creeping prepares us for the survivors, for the weeping, the wailing, the shaking in their shoes to hear something, anything, from us that will make it possible for them to make it through till morning. Those are the moments, my friend, when I have to think of something to say, doesn't matter where it comes from, that sounds as comfortable as small talk and as solid as the walls of St. Peter's. Believe me, Mario, that isn't easy. I've seen Reagan do it in the glare of international news media, and the man is utterly sincere."

"You know what they say about fakin' sincerity. Once you've got that down, you got it whipped."

"No no no. I'm telling you the man is not faking. He really is a master of consolation."

"Uh, if you don't mind, I'd rather have you be the master of consolation. I'd rather he spent a little more time studying the situation like before he put those Marines on the low ground in Lebanon, you know what I mean—what the hell are we talkin' about this for? Do you know?"

"What we're talking about this for, is that some people have a gift for saying the right things to people who are suffering very heavy grief—and we're also talking about how you cannot seem to bring yourself to, for want of a better expression, help your mother in her last moments. What you seem to be stuck on is feeling more sorrow for yourself than you are feeling compassion for her. You say you're afraid. Well, imagine how afraid she must be to be awake and to not be able to speak."

"If you're trying to make me feel guilty—"

"I am not."

"—if you're trying to make me feel guilty, you're doin' a hell of a job."

"I am not trying to make you feel guilt. I am trying to make you understand that your mother's predicament is much more compelling than your own, I mean, at the moment."

"You succeeded," Balzic said, emptying his glass and standing. "I'm in the wrong place. I gotta go."

"Mario, honestly, I had no intention of making you feel guilt. I thought we were just talking."

"Father, nobody just talks to a priest, just like nobody just talks to a cop. I don't care who we are, you and me, I don't care how well I know you, how much I like you, you're a priest. I call you 'Father.' I'm older than you and I call you 'Father.' I have never called you by your first name. I don't even know what it is. Doesn't that tell you somethin'? You tell me that I'm feelin' sorrier for myself than I am feelin' compassion for my mother, I'm not gonna sit here and act like we're talkin' about somebody else. That hits me in my guts because you're a priest tellin' me what I'm supposed to be doin', 'cause as long as I've been alive one priest or another has been tellin' me how to behave. I can't just turn that off and pretend I'm in some kind of group therapy. . . . Maybe five years from now—if we're both alive—we can talk about this without bein' involved, but Father, I could no more do that now than I could—hell, I don't know—play a harmonica."

Balzic started for the door. "Uh, listen, if that lady calls back, put a hook into her."

"How am I supposed to do that, exactly?"

"I don't know. Tell her she's not responsible for her kid's actions, just her kid. She can take credit for givin' him life, she doesn't have to take the blame for every stupid-ass thing he does." Balzic threw up his hands. "Lay some guilt on her, man. That's what you're good at. If Rockin' Horse Ronnie's a master at consolation, who's better at makin' guilt than a priest? That's what Mo Valcanas told me one time: The principal result of four thousand years of the Judeo-Christian tradition is guilt."

"Oh come on."

"I'm just tellin' you what he said."

"If he's sprung himself free from religion, why is he drunk so much?"

Balzic held up his hands and shook his head. "How the hell do I know? I'm just tellin' you what he said. I didn't say I agreed with him. Listen, I really gotta go. In my case, *one* of the results of the tradition is you made me feel guilty as hell about being here instead of up the hospital. Uh, Father, maybe this is no, uh, you should excuse the expression, consolation, but someplace I heard that nobody can make you feel anything you don't already feel."

The priest rolled his eyes. "I think I'll have another splash of wine on that one."

"Okay, so it wasn't the most intelligent thing anybody ever said. Aw never mind. I gotta go." He motioned for the priest to stay where he was. "I know how to get out of here. Just get a hook into that woman, okay?"

* * * * *

Back at the hospital, Balzic found nothing but frustration. His wife had left for reasons no one knew anything about, Dr. James had returned to his office to see patients, and all the nurses were carting out all their standard responses to standard questions asked by members of the immediate family. Balzic knew it was nurse-speak, and he knew, furthermore, that it was no different from doctor-speak or lawyer-speak or cop-speak. It was nurse-speak intended to make a parent or spouse or child feel confident that things were being done without ever saying specifically what those things were. Balzic couldn't blame the nurses for doing to him what he'd done hundreds of times to others; what he wanted to do was call a truce, say the game was suspended for a while because he was serious and his mother's condition was serious and he wasn't just some anxious irritable guy. He was for real and his mother was for real and he wanted to know for real how his mother was.

"She's doing just fine." "She's resting." "Doctor said she was lookin' real good." "As soon as the medication has a chance to work, you'll be able to see the change yourself."

Balzic wanted to throw chairs. Instead, he tried making a deal: "Hey, look, you don't BS me now about my mother, I promise not to BS anybody ever again in life, okay? Just cut all the syrupy crap and tell me what's goin' on, okay?"

"Doctor will be back tomorrow morning. 'Course, you could

call him at his office if you really think you have to talk to him."
"I don't think you have to worry. If there was a real problem,
doctor wouldn't have left. He's a really fine person, he's not just
a fine doctor, which he is, don't get me wrong. . . ."

Balzic went into his mother's room. Her eyes were closed, her
mouth was open, her breathing was coming in raspy spurts.
Sometimes she sounded like she was snoring; other times she
sounded like she couldn't get her breath.

Balzic couldn't remember ever seeing her this weak and
helpless. She looked so small, it was as though she was losing
height and weight before his eyes, as though she was dying by
inches and ounces. He knew that what he was thinking about,
what he was seeing, made no sense. He also knew that what he
was feeling was as true as anything he'd ever felt. He was
watching his mother die and there wasn't a goddamned thing
he could do about it and he was so frightened that his mouth
tasted the way it did when he awoke every morning, dry and
metallic, and his hands and feet were getting cold and his heart
was starting to hammer and he was breathing through his
mouth. . . .

He had to sit down. He was dizzy and his pulses were
pounding in his ears. He knew if he didn't slow his breathing
down, he was going to pass out. So he started to count, up to
eight on the inhale, to eight again on the exhale, racing through
all the good scenes in his mind about his mother . . . five, six,
seven, eight . . . his mother coming in from the garden, her
left hand holding the bottom of her apron up to her stomach
and stepping to the sink, spilling a dozen sweet peppers out
of her apron into the sink. Soon after, she put peppers,
onions, and garlic in oil in a cast-iron pan, simmering them
until the peppers were just softened, and then she heaped them
on a slice of bread from Mancini's Bakery, topped it with
another slice, and put it on a plate for him . . . one, two,
three, four . . . when he was small and fascinated by the blue
chips she put into the wringer-washer—"bluing," she called
it—and the smell of chlorine was so strong it made him sneeze,
but he loved to watch it dissolve in the back-and-forth motion of
the washing machine . . . five, six, seven, eight . . . the
washer was in the cellar of the house that had the dirt floor and

every Monday she smelled like old, damp dirt and chlorine . . . one, two, three, four . . . one time he pestered her so much she forgot herself and ran two fingers into the wringer; she just looked surprised and never made a sound until she backed the wringer handle up enough to free her fingers and then she beat her hand against her thigh and screamed at him to go outside and play . . . five, six, seven, eight . . . that wasn't one of the best times, that was one of the worst . . . but the best was always in the kitchen, when she was browning garlic in olive oil, the smell that seemed to come out of her instead of the pot . . . "I can't quit countin' now, I ain't gonna faint. . . ."

He wasn't. He knew that as surely as he knew she was going to die.

He sat up. Stood up. Something was not right. There was a steady whine. He looked at the EKG monitor, then at his mother. There was a straight line on the monitor; her mouth was open, her chin jutting up, her eyelids slits. All this took a second to register. He lurched to the door and bellowed something indescribable and then wheeled around and lunged to her side, but before he could even begin cardiopulmonary resuscitation, he was shoved aside by three nurses and a doctor. Somebody told him to "please wait outside."

Ten minutes later, the doctor came out. He seemed to Balzic to be hardly old enough to shave.

"I'm very sorry," he said. "We did everything we know how to do. It wasn't enough. I'm sorry."

Balzic nodded once or twice. He felt his face pursing, he felt his sighs coming one after another, he felt his eyes lock onto some point about three feet in front of him; and then, when he tried to look at the younger man to speak to him, he felt his eyelids drop like heavy wet cloths, and he could not think of a single word to say.

"If you want to be alone with her," the doctor said after a moment, "it's okay."

Balzic nodded several times and the heavy wet cloths over his eyes lifted and he stepped gingerly into the room. He shuffled to the bed and leaned over and took up his mother's right hand and kissed it. Then he bent down and kissed her on the lips.

"Jesus Christ, Ma . . . Jesus Christ . . . who am I gonna call when the nuns pick on me now?"

Someone came rushing in then and he heard, "Oh shit. Oh shit shit shit. . . ."

Balzic turned to see Ruth sobbing and swearing.

"She never woke up, baby," he said, putting his arm around her shoulders. "She never said a word. I was just sittin' there and I heard somethin' funny and I looked up and there was just a straight line on the thing over there, and they came in and worked on her real hard for about ten minutes but she was . . . gone."

". . . shit shit shit . . ." Ruth reached down and tried to push a lock of hair behind her mother-in-law's ear. It stuck out at an odd angle and resisted Ruth's attempts. "I should've been here, Mar, I was here the whole time except for this . . . I should've been here. . . ."

"It's okay," he said. "I was here."

"It's not okay. I should've been here. Where did I have to go that was so goddamn important? I don't even know why I left."

"One of us was here, it's okay. It is. Really."

Ruth shook her head emphatically from side to side. "I told myself I'd be here and when the time came I wasn't."

"She never woke up, Ruth. She never said a word."

"I don't care. I promised myself I'd be here and I wasn't and I can't even remember why I thought something was so goddamn important I had to leave. . . ."

One of the nurses came in and asked them to leave. "There are things we have to do now."

"Just give us another minute," Balzic said.

They used it all, and it was very long, that minute, and then they went home.

*   *   *   *   *

Of all the things Balzic had ever done in his life, none made his knees quiver more than walking into the basement of Bruno's Funeral Home to select a coffin for his mother. He and Ruth followed Sal Bruno around for ten minutes as he stopped at the various coffins and explained their features and prices. Balzic heard not a word.

He stopped and pulled Ruth's sleeve. "Do you know what he's been sayin'?"

"No," she said.

He turned to Sal Bruno, who stood with his hands folded behind his back.

"Sallie," Balzic said, "I can't do this. I don't know how much money my mother had, I haven't looked at her will yet. I think we should've done that first, but I'm all outta sequence, you know what I mean? I don't know what the hell's goin' on. I want you to do this. You pick it out, okay? Do this for me, okay? Please. Just remember I'm not loaded, okay?"

Sal Bruno rocked back and looked at his shoes. He cleared his throat and licked his lips. When he looked up, tears were streaming down his cheeks. His voice cracked when he started to speak, so he closed his eyes for a moment, then he began again.

"Mario, I will be proud to do this. But not for you. For her. See . . . if it wasn't for her, I wouldn't have this business. See, forty years ago, nobody would come to me and I didn't know why. And I asked around and I asked and I asked, and little by little it came out. My mother, uh, she wasn't married when I was born. These people . . . they didn't want a bastard doing this—even though my mother and my father eventually got married and even though it wasn't my fault, still, you remember how they were? A bastard was a bastard, like a criminal. And it was your mother who went around to all of them, the Sons of Italy, the Christopher Columbus Club, the Monte Grappa League, the Catholic Daughters, the Rosary Altar Society, the priests, the nuns.

"Mario, you pick out whatever you like, none of this is gonna cost you anything—"

"Oh you can't do that."

"Mario, this is for her, this is not for you. She made my life for me. If it wasn't for her going around telling everybody they were foolish for not coming to me, they would've never come to me. Do you understand what I'm saying to you?"

"Yes, I think so."

"I should've just told you, I should've told you I'd take care of everything. Believe me, the pope won't get any better than I give your mother. I owe her everything, honest. And I don't know any other way to repay her. So let me do it, okay? I need your permission, I won't feel right without your permission."

Balzic looked at Ruth and then at Bruno. "You have it. It's just a shame she—I mean, she won't know."

"Oh she knew. I told her as soon as I found out what she'd done. She just laughed a little bit and said she hoped I wouldn't get a chance real soon. But I promised her. I said if I'm alive I'll take care of everything. She just laughed, but I don't think there was any doubt in her mind that I meant it."

Balzic shrugged again. "I guess that only leaves the obituary."

"Yes," Bruno said. "Let's go upstairs to my office and I'll take all that down and I'll make sure it's in tomorrow's paper."

"Just one thing about that," Balzic said, holding up his left index finger and jabbing the air several times. "As long as Murray was alive, he used to make sure all the obituaries were right. He used to have a sign up over his desk that said something like, 'Most people only get their names in the paper when they're born, when they die, when they get arrested. The least we can do is make sure their names are spelled right.' But I hear the guy that runs that place now, he doesn't give a shit about that. In fact, I hear he took the sign down. So you tell 'em they don't get my mother's name right, I'll make 'em wish they were sellin' shoes."

"I understand, Mario. Believe me, I understand. And I'll tell them."

*　　*　　*　　*　　*

After they had given Sal Bruno all the information they had for the obituary, they stepped outside into a dull drizzle. Coming up the walk from the parking lot was Father Marrazo, his head canted away from the rain, his pace urgent.

He spoke to both, embraced Ruth, and gave his sympathy. "Whatever I can do, please ask. She was one of my favorite people. You want special music, just say it."

"Thank you Father. Very much."

The priest cleared his throat, pursed his lips, and inhaled noisily. "Mario, Ruth," he said after a moment, "I think you should know that your mother's passing is not, or cannot be, merely a passing. Uh, because of her stature in the parish, because of her influence in many groups—I don't know exactly how to put this—but because she was so highly respected, and because so many people knew her, her, uh, her passing is going to take on a meaning of its own. Already, I've had telephone requests for masses and rosaries. The wakes are being planned, the vigils—it's almost out of your hands. No, that's not what I mean to say—do you know what I mean?"

"Her friends want to honor her," Ruth said.

"Exactly," the priest said.

"And we have to let them," she said.

"Yes! Exactly."

"We can do that," Ruth said. "Mar? Can we do that?"

"Sure. Why not? Just so they give us some time—"

"Oh of course, Mario, of course. But in this very short time since I heard the news, my phone has not stopped. And it's going to get bigger. Really."

Balzic shrugged. "I know she's got friends, and I, uh, hey, let 'em do what they wanna do. Can't stop 'em anyway."

"Good. Good," the priest said. "Now. We have another problem. She's in my car."

"Who is?" Ruth said.

"Mario? The woman? Remember—with the son?"

"Oh, Father, come on," Ruth said.

"I'm only doing what Mario asked me to do. He told me to throw a hook into her. Ruth, I'm sorry, but . . . this woman has a problem too."

"I don't give a goddamn about her problem. My best friend just died. She's also my husband's mother."

"Mario, she's in my car. Ruth, let's go for a walk, okay?"

"I don't want to go for a walk."

"Please, Ruth," the priest said. "C'mon. Let's walk."

Ruth's shoulders sagged, then stiffened. "If you weren't a priest, I'd smack you one. Well, let's go. C'mon before I change my mind."

Ruth took the priest by the arm and led him off. She turned

95

and said, "Don't take all goddamn day with whoever it is. I need some wine. I'm hungry."

"Okay, okay," Balzic said. "It'll depend on her."

"Well tell her to hurry up. I'm sick of this crap."

"Ruth," the priest said, "it's not something he can help."

"Oh shut up and walk. You want to walk? Then walk."

Balzic closed his eyes for a long moment, trying to find his professional attitude or what, under the circumstances, would pass for it. But he couldn't remember what a professional attitude was. Worse, of all the thoughts rocketing around in his mind, not one was about the woman he was walking toward the parking lot to meet.

"Mister Chief? Over here," came the woman's voice.

Balzic took some moments trying to fix the sound. When he spotted her finally, she was hunkered down on the passenger side of the front seat of the priest's Oldsmobile, the top of her head just visible behind the dashboard.

Balzic went over and clambered in behind the steering wheel. "Before we start, ma'am, I want to tell you my mother just died, so if I seem a little spacey, uh, I hope you understand."

"Father told me on the way up here. I'm real—you have my sympathy."

"Thank you. Did you know my mother?"

"No. But Father told me she was a real wonderful person. I guess she would be to have a son who would grow up to be a chief of police."

"I beg your pardon?"

"Well I mean you wouldn't be a police chief if your mother was a bad person. You wouldn't have a model to—a person to model yourself after."

"Oh. I see what you're gettin' at." Balzic studied her face again, trying to decide why she lacked definition, why she looked as though she might vanish while he watched her. It was as though she estimated herself so poorly that it was contagious, that another person could sit within arm's length and see just the barest outline of a person, constantly ready to disappear at the first hint of danger.

Balzic said it quietly: "Your husband beats you up, doesn't he?"

She immediately reached for the door handle.

Balzic put his hand on her shoulder. "It was just a question. It wasn't an attack."

When she turned back to him her face was pasty, grayish. She didn't take her hand off the door handle.

"He does not," she said without conviction.

"Yes he does. And you're petrified what he's gonna do when he finds out you been talkin' to a cop."

"I'm not talking about him! Why should I be scared?"

"I know you're not talkin' about him. I'm the one who brought it up. But I think what's goin' on here is you're caught between talkin' about your son and what your husband's gonna do when he finds out you've been talkin' about your son—is that right or not?"

She took a long time to answer. "I guess."

"There are things you can do about that, you know."

"I don't—I don't want to talk about him . . . I want to ask you about something else."

"Go ahead and ask."

"Just—just for the sake of talkin', okay? Just let's pretend for a minute, okay?"

"Okay."

"So okay. So say a person came home and found another person all covered with blood and . . . say that other person was all hung over . . . say that other person was really really drunk the night before and couldn't remember nothin' . . . nothin' at all—except drinkin' a whole lot of beer."

"Ma'am, I believe I already told you about the possibilities here."

"I know you did, but I think we were talking like it was an accident. . . ."

"And it's not an accident?"

"I didn't say that."

"I don't want to put words in your mouth, ma'am, honest, I don't, but I think it would help us both if you would come up with a little more detail, if you follow me."

She eyed him carefully. She looked out the windshield two or three times and each time turned back to him to search his face, all the while chewing the inside of her lower lip.

"Did you respect your mother?"

Balzic nodded.

"I mean really respect her? Did you honor her like it says?"

"I tried."

"Did she respect you?"

"I think so, yes."

"Did she—"

"Ma'am, if you don't quit talkin' about my mother, I'm gonna start bawlin'—"

"Yes, but I want to know. I have to know. Did she respect you? Did she protect you, for instance?"

"Ma'am, I—I don't know how to tell you what you want to know. All I know is, I never felt this weak. And I guess the only reason you feel like this is 'cause you don't have your mother anymore."

She chewed the inside of her cheek and sighed noisily. "I'm trying to protect—I'm trying to be a good person, a good mother, but I don't know what a good mother is. My mother died with I was five and her sisters raised me and . . . and all I ever learned from them was I didn't know the meaning of *grateful*. It was like if it wasn't for me both of them would've been in the movies or somethin'—you know what I mean?"

Balzic nodded several times. "I think so."

"Well when my husband came along, he could've been a—God I don't know what he could've been, anything, a boy cheerleader, a band sissy, all he had to do was just listen to me for five minutes and I'd've followed him anywhere, that's how ready I was to run. And it didn't start—it really didn't—till after, uh, our little boy, till after he was born. And then he . . . he didn't . . . he quit listenin' to me after that. . . ."

"Is that when he started hittin' you?"

She took a long time to reply. "It wasn't till he got laid off. But that came real soon. I mean he was born and then 'bout four months later, Rich got laid off . . . that's when it . . . that was the start."

"Listen, ma'am, people used to treat this kind of thing like it was between the husband and wife, you know? And it wasn't something for the police to do but go in and calm things down. But that's not true, well, some places it still is, but lots of departments are handlin' it like it's assault and battery between strangers. The wife doesn't have to sign the information against her husband. The police officer makes an arrest on his own judgment that a crime has taken place, you follow that?"

"You think so, huh?"

"I know so, ma'am."

"And whatta you think happens after he gets outta jail? You think it makes any difference whether he goes to jail 'cause a cop said so or 'cause I said so? The reason he's in jail is 'cause he hit me, it don't matter nothin' whose word it was got him in jail."

"You'd be surprised how many men quit gettin' so handsy after they spend a couple of weeks locked in."

"Oh yeah? Well maybe you oughta talk to the women whose husbands don't fit in with your idea. I think you're the one'd be surprised how many husbands get a whole lot madder at their wives after they been in jail. One of the women I used to talk to at the women's center, her husband come out of jail and wasn't out two hours and he just beat her to death. Right in front of her two kids."

"I remember that one, ma'am, but I think you'll find that for every husband like that, there are fifty who suddenly get civilized in jail—as far as their wives are concerned, that is."

"Well, that's not a whole bunch of consolation to the lady who's dead now, is it?"

"Lady, I'm not givin' anybody perfect odds on anything. I'm just tellin' you that sometimes you have to play the best odds you get, even if they're not real promising."

"Is that the best you can do?"

"Lady, I ain't God. I'm a cop who's gettin' real close to lookin' for another line of work. I'm just tryin' to get out with my buns and my brain in more or less one piece. Right now, I'll settle for my buns bein' in one piece. So if you got somethin' you want to tell me, you better do it before you have to start talkin' to somebody who busts you for obstructin' justice and really makes you miserable."

"Does what? You mean arrests me?"

"Yes, ma'am."

"For doin' what now?"

"For obstruction of justice."

"Why?"

"Because they'd get tired of talkin' to you. They'd get tired of bein' tested. They'd get tired of dealin' with all the hypotheticals you throw up, and they'd say, Look, lady, either you tell us what you wanna tell us or we're gonna go talk to a judge and he'll make you tell us. And believe me, you think you have problems now? They're nothin' to the problems you'll have when you try to tell a judge that you're tryin' to figure out what's the right thing to do. He'll be sympathetic for about five minutes. And after three minutes, believe me, he'll start lookin' at his watch. You understand any of this?"

She nodded slowly.

"Believe me, ma'am, I don't want to hassle you, but I'm not in the most patient mood right now. My mother's gone. You're a mother and you got a decision to make. But somebody else had a mother, too. She's never gonna be a candidate for Mother of the Year, that's for sure, but she was somebody's mother."

She looked away, outside the passenger window. Then she looked at her hands in her lap. Then she began to chew on her right thumbnail.

"What's your name, ma'am?"

"Not yet," she said.

"Well how 'bout your son? He have a name?"

"Not yet, I said." She was barely whispering.

"How 'bout your husband? What's his name? Where's he work? What's he do? Does he have a job? What's he do when he isn't beatin' you up?"

"Please," she said, shaking her head from side to side, still chewing on her thumbnail. "I can't." She heaved a quavery sigh. "I can't do it yet."

"You're just prolongin' your discomfort, ma'am. The longer you put it off, the more complicated it's gonna look. You'll start seein' sides to this that'll paralyze ya, if you let it."

"I'm already paralyzed. I never been so scared in my life."

"Uh-ha. I'm sure you are, ma'am. Maybe I oughta tell ya what happened."

"No don't. Please. I ain't ready—I'm not, honest to God I ain't."

"I think you pretty much know, ma'am. I think you pretty much guessed what happened."

"No I didn't. I didn't guess nothin'."

"Well, then I think I oughta tell ya—"

"Oh God please no. Please please no."

"Lady, you're lettin' yourself get hung out to dry. You're lettin' your husband and your son put you out there on that line."

"You don't know nothin'," she said sharply. It was the first time she had even slightly raised her voice.

"Ma'am, I've seen women like you before. Many, many times. They think—they actually believe they deserved what's happenin' to 'em. They let themselves be used and misused by their husbands, and then they let their sons use 'em and misuse 'em. They think if they don't allow themselves to be used, their husbands and sons are gonna go away. But, lady, nothin' you ever did or nothin' you ever thought you did makes it okay to be walked over."

"I am not bein' walked on."

"Lady, you got all the signs. The fact that you're here now, debatin' whether to tell me is like neon on your forehead. I have to close my eyes not to see it. It's fluorescent pink and it says 'sucker' in capital letters."

"Does not," she grumbled into her chest. Her breathing was becoming audible.

"Oh it does too. And you got a bulls-eye on your back right under another neon sign that says DON'T KICK ME. And every day you wake up you can't understand how come your dupa's sore, and you keep waitin' for somebody to pat you on the head and give you a hug and say, there, there, everything's just peachy, you've been a good girl, here's some money, go buy some candy, and you can't understand why nobody does.

"Lady, I'm here to tell ya, the more you do for people like your husband, the more they kick you in the butt. They think it's part of their job description: get married, screw, kick butt."

She lifted her chin off her chest and stared at him, horrified. "You're so . . . vulgar. The priest said you were nice, but you're . . . real vulgar."

Balzic rubbed his mouth and sighed. "Lady, I'm tryin' to cut

101

right to the chase here and I'm all out of patience. My guts hurt I miss my mother so much. I don't have time to hold your hand and walk you through this. I probably shouldn't even be talkin' to you. I probably should be lettin' you talk to somebody who has a lot more patience than I have right now, but here you are and so am I, so . . . so listen to me."

"Your son needs to come in and explain—"

"I never said it was my son. I never said anything about him."

"The priest did. You told the priest, the priest told me. I just want to ask you one question, lady. You can take as long as you want to answer. You can take till next Sunday, I don't care, but sooner or later you're gonna have to deal with this: Your son carry a folding knife, about so long?" Balzic held up his hands about eight or nine inches apart.

Her eyes grew wide. "How do you know that?" she whispered.

"I don't know it, lady. It wasn't a statement, it was a question. What I do know is there's a body in the hospital pathology lab with a least twenty-nine knife wounds in it and—"

Her hands flew to her mouth and she sucked in a breath. She spun and fumbled with the door handle, threw her shoulder into it to pop it open, squirmed outside, and bolted stiffly away, her arms like boards against her sides.

Balzic watched her go and shook his head. He never even thought about going after her.

He heard someone talking and turned and saw Ruth and Father Marrazo coming near.

He got out of the car and waited.

"Is she gone?" Ruth said. "Good. We have to go. I want to be home when Marie and Emily get there."

"What happened?" the priest asked.

"I leaned on her too hard and she ran."

"What did she say? Anything?"

"She said as little as possible, but it was enough."

"Mario, can we please go home?"

"Enough? Enough for what? What enough?"

"Hey, we'll talk about it some other time, okay? All I wanna say is this: She'll be back. And when she does, try to get a name or an address. I know it'll be hard but—"

"Mario, please?"

"See ya, Father. Thanks for comin'.".

"What're you thanking him for? He brought that woman."

"Ruth, gimme a break, okay? We're goin', okay? Try to help me out on this, Father, okay? I'll see ya."

"I'll give you a break. Just give me a break and take me home. I want to be there when the girls come."

"I'm takin' you home, Ruth. And the last time I heard anything about it, both of our daughters had their own keys to the house. I'm sure they can find their way in."

"That's not the point."

Right, Balzic thought. It wasn't the point. And quibbling about it was going to turn it into something way beside the point, into something neither one of them needed, so he was quiet all the way home.

*　　*　　*　　*　　*

Once home, they took turns answering the phone or the door. Ladies from the neighborhood, most Balzic didn't know by name, started showing up with food or Mass cards or both. Within an hour, the refrigerator in the kitchen was full, and Balzic was going up and down to the old Sears Coldspot fridge in the cellar.

"Where we gonna have the people afterward? We can't have 'em here."

"What's wrong with the Sons of Italy Hall?"

"Who calls them? Whatta you say—I want to rent the hall for a wake?"

"Why not?"

"Sounds goofy . . . sound like you're gettin' ready to have a celebration."

"We are. We're going to celebrate her life—you get the phone, I'll get the door."

What he got, after he picked up the phone, was a glass in the kitchen and a carafe full of chablis from the fridge.

"It's me, Mario. Carlucci."

"Hey, Rugs. What's up?"

"I just heard and I want to express my sympathy. And I want to tell you that if there's anything I can do, please ask me."

"Thanks, Rugs. Since you brought it up, your father's funeral, didn't you have the thing afterwards down the SOI?"

"Yeah. Why?"

"Well who took care of that?"

"Jeez I don't know. I think my uncle. But if that's what you want me to do, I'll check it out, I'll let you know as soon as I find out."

"Hey, Rugs, thanks, that'll really help."

"Say no more. I consider it an honor. She was like family, you know? I called her Aunt Marie."

"I know, Rugs. Thanks again. I'll see ya."

"Oh wait. Remember that guy you asked me to check out? The Lutheran preacher?"

"Yeah."

"Well he isn't one. He was defrocked last year. But I couldn't get any details unless I had a court order. And the guy I talked to, this Reverend Lucius Mitinger, he said they might not tell me even then. He said there'd have to be—how'd he put it? 'An overwhelming legal compulsion,' something like that."

"Okay, Rugs, good job. And thanks for the other stuff, too."

"The other stuff is my pleasure, Mario. I'll get back to you in a coupla hours, maybe less. I gotta go home first and take care of my mother. I almost forgot. Yesterday she told me, 'Why can't you be on television? They make millions. Everybody in television makes millions. You could do that. All you have to do is talk good. You don't have to be a stupid cop the rest of your life.' I just thought you'd like to hear my mother's latest plan for how I'm supposed to get rich."

"Believe me, Rugs, under other circumstances, I'd be howlin', 'cause that's funny, but you can see that I'm not. But that's good. Just talk good, huh? That's all you gotta do."

"Yeah. That's it. Okay, Mario. Talk to you later, soon as I know something."

The more people phoned, the more people came, the blurrier it all became for Balzic, because all the words, all the sympathy, all the expressions of condolence started to dissolve into the next one, so that he saw no particular faces, heard no specific words, and was conscious only of the dizzy feeling of being unconnected to any of the people who felt compelled to help him and his family.

"Hello? Who is this?"

"Mario."

"I'ma sorry. I'ma Mrs. Ciamocco. I knowa you mother sincea 1940. I gonna pray for her. You too."

"Thank you."

"Don'ta worry. She'sa already witha God."

"Thank you."

He hung up and was befuddled by the hushed conversation that filled the living room. There were twenty women in the entryway, the living room, and under the arch leading into the kitchen. He went to refill his glass and had to walk sideways, slipping between women he recalled seeing at every wedding, christening, funeral, and church supper he'd ever taken his mother to, but he would not have a bet a dime on his memory of their names.

A woman was bent over, peering into the fridge. She was barely five feet tall and boney and she was dressed as though ready for church.

"You're Mario?" she said as he reached around her to get the chablis.

"Yes. Who are you?"

"You don't remember me?"

"No."

"I'm Mrs. Parenti. We used to live in the next block? Then we moved to Westfield Township? You don't remember?"

"How'd you hear about my mother so fast if you live in the township?"

"My sister called me. Don't you have any cream?"

"Any what?"

"Cream? For the coffee."

"We use milk."

"I'll drink it black then. So you don't remember us, huh? Not even my husband? You arrested him once. He used to have chickens, and that stupid Polock Blashinsky kept calling you and complaining until you finally came and arrested him."

"Uh, it's startin' to come back, yeah. So how's your husband?"

"Oh, he died. Right after we moved. He's been gone now, it'll be fifteen years next month. I'm real sorry about your mother—did I say that?"

"Probably, yeah. Thanks."

"She was a wonderful person. Really."

"Thank you. I know."

He turned away, holding the carafe and his glass aloft until he could sidestep to the sink, five feet away, and refill his glass. There were half again as many women in the kitchen as there were in the living room, and he didn't remember one of their names. He sidled back to the fridge, put the carafe back inside, and then eased his way back toward the phone table in the corner of the living room. He thought for a moment that his throat was swelling shut. It was an old and miserably familiar sensation, always close by when he was in the middle of a funeral crowd. Then somebody had their arms around his neck and was sobbing quietly into his chest and he felt himself recoiling. Then the person pulled her blond hair back and the face under that looked strangely familiar to him but it didn't go with the blond hair.

"Daddy, I'm sorry, I'm so sorry. . . ."

Daddy?

"Marie?"

"Yes." Her eyes were raw and the corners of her lips were sticking together.

"You don't have blond hair. Since when do you have blond hair? You had black hair since the day you were born."

"I dyed it."

"What d'you do that for? Jesus I didn't even recognize you."

"Just got bored, I don't know. What happened? Never mind about me. What happened?"

Balzic shrugged. "I don't know. Today I was sittin' with her and I looked up and all of a sudden that little EKG monitor, right next to her bed, the line just went straight across. No more up and down, just flat. And they worked on her for, I don't know, ten, fifteen minutes and she was . . . gone."

"Oh, Daddy, I'm so sorry. I just talked to her three days ago. I told her I was coming home this weekend. I asked her to tell me I wasn't crazy, I just dyed my hair, and she thought that was so funny. She asked me all about it, how I did it, she said she always wanted to know how women dyed their hair and I was the first person she ever felt it was okay to ask. I had to tell her my roommate did it so I didn't know how to do it, but I said we could go see Julie—the lady who does her hair?"

"Julie?"

"Yeah. Julie Nocera. She's right over there. By the stove. With the hoop earrings. God I'm gonna miss her."

"Me too."

"Where's Em?"

"Didn't she come home with you?"

"Daddy, I don't live with Em anymore, remember? I live in Pittsburgh. I haven't lived with Em for two years. Geez, Daddy."

"Hey, kiddo, I'm a little frazzled, okay? Listen, I gotta get outta here. I can't stand all this, all this . . . quiet noise. I'm goin' to Muscotti's. Tell your mother the next time you see her, okay?"

"Daddy, you can't leave now. She needs you now."

"Listen, she's been snipin' at me all day. Better for both of us if I wasn't around for a while, believe me."

"I don't think you should go, Daddy. I don't think that's fair."

"Marie," he said, sighing, "I don't wanna talk about fair right now. I wanna go someplace where I don't have to listen to all these women reminiscin'. All this whisperin's givin' me a goddamn headache."

He kissed her on the head again, and then he shuffled and slipped between the women, saying thanks for coming, thanks for being here, thanks for bringing the food, thanks thanks thanks, and then he was out the front door and into his cruiser and headed for Muscotti's.

Mo Valcanas was at the jukebox swaying to the rhythm of Ray Charles singing "Georgia on My Mind." Vinnie was on the phone swearing at the top of his lungs that he was going to quit so help him if he had to work one more double shift, fair was fair and right was right and loyalty was loyalty, ". . . but I ain't no donkey." He slammed down the phone so hard it bounced out of its cradle and clattered to the floor.

"Do you mind?" Valcanas said, squinting over his shoulder at

Vinnie. "I'm trying to get full value for my musical money here."

"I got your full value right here," Vinnie said, pointing at his crotch. "Hey, Mario, I'm sorry about your mother. You have my sympathy."

"Where's Dom? Thank you. Thank you very much. Doesn't he work anymore?"

"Fuck Dom. I just told his old lady, I ain't no fuckin' donkey. This is the third day this week I'm workin' double shifts. He's like he's goin' through the change of life, you know? He got retired, see? So all of a sudden, he can't do nothin', so 'cause he can't do nothin' 'cause he got retired, all of a sudden I'm a fuckin' machine, you know? Put a quarter in me, wind me up, and I go all fuckin' day. I ain't gettin' no fuckin' younger either, you know? So what happened to your mother?"

"Mother," Valcanas said, turning away from the jukebox and coming to the bar, "a film on the surface of alcoholic beverages during the process of fermentation, a more glorious word never existed. What happened to whose mother?"

Balzic nodded rapidly many times, his head down. "Gone," was the only word he could get out.

Valcanas licked his lips slowly. Then he brought out his wallet and put three twenties on the bar. He made a circular motion with his hand, as though to say, pour for the three of us and keep them coming.

"Put it away, Greek," Vinnie said. "Your money's no good here. That fuckin' Dom's gonna make me work till I drop, Mario's mother passes on, may she rest in peace, we're gonna drink on Dom."

Valcanas nodded somberly. "Vinnie, I give you more than your share of malevolent manure, but I have to admit that sometimes you have a remarkable nobility of spirit."

"What's that mal what?"

"Malevolent manure. Bad shit."

"Why didn't you say so? So what's it gonna be, Mario? How 'bout let's break into the old prick's private cabinet, whatta ya say? Whatta ya want, red or white?"

"Red," Balzic said.

"Hey, he got some stuff here he paid a hundred and

eighty-some bucks a case for. Gattinara. From the Piedmont. Lemme pop the cork on some of those, huh?" He ducked away into the kitchen.

Valcanas put his hand on Balzic's back. "The only finer woman who lived was my mother. She died four years ago, and every day I wake up I expect her to call to ask me why I haven't come to see her."

Vinnie came hustling back, three lead-crystal glasses in his left hand, three bottles in his right hand. He set the glasses on the bar and the bottles underneath on the shelf. While he was opening one of the bottles, he nodded toward the glasses and said, "If we're gonna drink the good shit, we're gonna drink it outta the Lenox glasses too, right? Hey, Vinnie's first rule of life is, you don't drink the good shit outta cheap glasses."

"When'd it happen?" Valcanas said.

"I don't know, this afternoon. I feel like I'm in this huge cardboard box, it's all full of those Styrofoam hickeys, about the size of prunes, you know? There's eight zillion of 'em in there and I'm in up to my hips and I can't make any progress no matter which way I go. And then somehow I do make it to the side of the box and I can't get a handhold.

"My mother's dead, my wife's pissed off at me, some faggot got himself stuck about thirty times, some woman thinks her son did this stickin' but she's too scared to talk about it, and some goddamned defrocked preacher is runnin' around bitchin' about pornography, and my house is full of women whisperin'. You know the sound of women whisperin' can make you instantly crazy? You guys know that?"

"Absolutely," Vinnie said. "And they always show up when somebody dies. You never see 'em no place else, but when somebody dies, there they are. They got their arms fulla food and they're all takin' under their breath."

"The reason *you* never see them is 'cause *you* never go to church," Valcanas said. "That's where they are. That's why they always show up when somebody dies. They hear right away. And that's what they do, that's their job—make food and take it to the family."

"I guess *you* go to church, right? If ever there was a nonbelievin' sonofabitch, it's you."

Valcanas stepped back and bowed slightly. "Vinnie, I under-estimated you. First, nobility of spirit, and now perspicacity."

"C'mon, Greek. Talk fuckin' English, huh?"

"American. This noise we make is only remotely connected to English."

Vinnie filled the third glass and said, "English, American, whatever. Let's try this out."

They lifted their glasses and drank.

"Not bad, huh?" Vinnie said.

Balzic nodded many times. Valcanas said, "It would probably be a lot smoother if you'd given it some air for about a half-hour. You ought to open the other two bottles."

"You think we're gonna drink 'em all?"

"A man's mother dies once. Open 'em up, give 'em some air, we'll drink 'em. And if we don't, you can always put one in a doggy bag for me."

"So, uh, Panagios, for the sake of conversation, for gettin' my mind off all the rest, tell me, you ever try any porn cases?"

"Never on a question of what constituted obscenity, if that's what you want to know. Every one I've ever been involved in had to do with an illegal wiretap or some goofy zoning law. I've never tried one on the merits of what was obscene—and I hope I never do."

"Why?"

"Obscenity is like beauty, my man. All in the eye of the beholder. You can argue for years on what is or isn't and all you're gonna get is hoarse. Which is not to say there haven't been some splendid arguments in various cases. But even those are really all beside the point."

"What point is that?"

"Well, I forget which porn commission it was, but they issued their report during Nixon's first administration. And the majority report was that porn did not lead to anything but masturbation, you know, reading *Playboy* didn't cause you to go out and rape your sister or whatever. Anyway, Nixon said in so many words, well, we all know that's not true because if it was, then what would be the point of reading good books?

"And that's the thing nobody wants to consider. If Nixon's objection has merit, then the whole educational system of

Western civilization collapses, 'cause if you say that reading bad books does not make you do bad things, then how can anybody justify spending all that time and money to make people read good books if it isn't going to turn them into proper little citizens? See, porn has to make people do bad things, otherwise you'd have to dismiss all the schools as an irrelevant joke. But to say that reading good books creates only goodness and light is asinine when you consider how many lawyers have been sent to prison, or how many doctors have committed insurance fraud or killed their wives, or how many cops have turned sour.

"Besides, the thing all the porn police never reflect on, is what do you blame it on before the printing press was invented? Before the camera was invented? Do they actually believe nobody got sodomized before there were X-rated movies? There wasn't any cable TV in Sodom. These porn nuts have got everything backasswards. The events happen before the story gets told, not after. But people who believe in good books, hell, their whole existence is based on the book first, then life. And that's just turned-around bullshit, but you're never gonna convince them of that."

"Why not? Why can't they be convinced?"

"You really want to know about this? Or you just tryin' to dodge reality?"

"Both. I really do want to know about it, 'cause this defrocked preacher came to see me and bitched about the porn store and in a matter of hours, a body turns up behind the store and then he starts hollerin' about how one leads to the other, and I got spooked. I mean, I hate to admit it, but I did."

"Look, ax-grinders had purported to prove that watching violence leads to violence, that watching sex leads to sex. There are so many thousand incidents of murder by gunfire over a certain period on TV and that's why there are so many gun murders in America. But, see, they never explain why every person who watches TV hasn't committed a gun murder. If you say that merely by watching an event, you're then compelled to produce a similar event, then you have to explain why every person who watches that event doesn't also attempt to produce a similar event. But with true believers, these things are articles

111

of faith; you read skin magazines, you're gonna rape and sodomize, that's all there is to it."

"This may be too complicated for my brain at this time," Balzic said.

"It's sure as hell too complicated for mine," Vinnie said, refilling their glasses.

"It's not that complicated," Valcanas said. "But it's nowhere near as simple as the porn nuts make it."

"Well all these studies and commissions that say that porn leads to sex crimes, they all wrong?"

"Mario, up until the fifteenth century everybody believed the earth was flat and anybody who said otherwise was a heretic or a lunatic. You run into somebody who says the earth is flat now, whatta you do? I don't know about you, but I walk away as fast as I can, 'cause I know I'm talking to somebody whose elevator hasn't made it to the second floor."

"So, what you're tellin' me is, porn is just porn. It doesn't do anything either way."

"No no no, that's not what I'm sayin' at all. There are guys who read porn and get all out of joint and sodomize their kid sisters. What I'm saying is that logically, legally, the argument that porn is a contributing factor in every instance a sex crime is committed is a non sequitur. In the first place, it's a gross misunderstanding of the function of language—on two levels. As a matter of semantics it's a fundamental mistake to believe that the word *is* the thing it represents. That's also true of pictures, movies, painting, makes no difference. I can write the word 'whiskey' on a piece of paper until my hand goes numb, but that word is not drinkable, you get what I'm saying? I can take pictures of a glass of whiskey until my camera runs out of film, but I can't drink those pictures either."

"Yeah, but they make you wanna get a drink," Vince said.

"Only if I'm a drinker!"

"Well, yeah, but that's exactly what the porn police are sayin'—put the porn in the wrong hands and these guys go nuts."

"Mario, there isn't anybody walkin' around today—and I mean nobody—who can explain how the human brain works. You can get all the smartest research people into one room and what they'd say is, they have some decent theories about memory, for example, but they have no proof. They wouldn't dare say, yes, we know what memory is, how it works chemically, neurologically, and we know exactly why people remember, A, B, and C, but forget X, Y, and Z. There isn't a brain researcher alive who would dare make statements like that. But the porn cops, they make statements like that all the time: Jones reads *Playboy*, Jones rapes stepdaughter, therefore reading *Playboy* causes sex crimes. It's bad logic. It's confusion over semantics, over human motivation, and over law. Fact is, having sex with children at certain times in certain cultures was the thing to do. The Greeks, they know the treeks. Pederasty comes from a Greek word, comes from *pais*, which means 'child.' Now if you believe that all these guys were walkin' around in Athens one day and suddenly they saw this word written on a wall, *paiderastia*, and they all said, wow, we have to start doing that—well, that's just ridiculous. To think a person has to see a word for something or a picture of something before he does it just flies in the face of logic. Prisons are full of illiterate rapists."

By this time they were working on the second bottle of Gattinara and Balzic was feeling cottony around the edges. Vinnie had thrown everybody else out—had locked both doors, in fact—and Valcanas was continuing his theorizing.

". . . The whole goddamn argument is nothing but the farcical triumph of the advertising bastards anyway."

"Right," Balzic said thickly.

"The hustlers have got to be pattin' themselves on the back every time they see some porn cop stand up and thump on a pile of *Playboys*."

"Whyzat?" Vinnie said. "I like *Playboy*."

"Course you like *Playboy*. You like teeny girls with big tits. The question is whether you liked 'em before or after you ever heard of *Playboy*."

"Before, definitely before. I didn't need no fuckin' Hugh Shafner to tell me who I like. I ain't stupid."

"See, Mario? A perfect illustration. And it's Hefner, not Shafner."

"Whatever."

"What perfect illustration?"

113

"The advertising guys. They've got everybody in the Western world convinced that they create desire. *Them*. See, this is how those scuzzballs go into every goddamn meeting with the marketing guys and proclaim that advertisin' works. And the marketing guys tells the finance guys and the finance guys tell the vice presidents in charge of fleecing the shareholders how they have to have more money to spend on advertising because how else are they gonna—what the hell do they say? *Capture the market share*, some crap like that. And then you have the universities, see, they're givin' away Ph.D.s in motivational research, and they're out measuring how many times ladies blink at different boxes of soap 'cause they just *know* those women don't know one kind of soap from another without bein' told. And by whom?"

"Whom?"

"Them. Of course. You think the advertising industry is gonna stand around quietly while somebody says that words and pictures and movies *don't* create desire? Shit, their whole reason for being depends on everybody buying into that game. That's the game of this century."

"Maybe so. But it sounds to me like it proved its point. How many people you know just buy a newspaper to see what's on sale? I know a bunch of women, they only go to the movies to see what the actresses are wearin'. That's half the reason they watch TV."

"Mario, the point is not how many people fall for the con. A con is a con; doesn't matter how many people fall for it.

"The advertisers have conned a whole civilization into payin' them a lotta money to grease the gears of their machine, to keep them rich, and they do it on the premise that *their* words and *their* pictures create desire for *their* clients' products, and so naturally, anybody who buys into that hustle is gonna believe that it is not only true, but that it is true everywhere and for everybody. And that's just bullshit.

"You want to stop an ad guy in his tracks? Ask him how capitalism got started without TV commercials. You want to stop a porn cop? Ask him how Christianity got started without Bibles."

"Which came first?" Vinnie said. "The hustler or the sucker?"

"Well, in this case, there isn't any question about it. The testicles were there long before anybody had a word for 'em. Or a picture."

Balzic nodded heavily. All the wine he'd had at home plus the wine he was having now plus the fact that he'd not eaten since seven that morning were combining to sink his chin. But he was hanging on to what Valcanas was saying because he kept thinking there was something wrong.

"I always wanted to know why," he said.

"Why what?" said Valcanas.

"I think he's gettin' ready to crash and burn," said Vinnie.

"No I'm not."

"Read my lips. You're gettin' ready to crash. Your eyelids are practically on your cheeks. How long you been drinkin' today?"

"Read your own goddamn lips. What the hell's so interesting about them—they're so goddamn skinny nobody could print nothin' on 'em anyway."

"Maybe he's right," Valcanas said. "You do look pretty bad—"

"Hey fuck the both of ya. I'm not interested in your opinion of how drunk I am. What I wanna know is this: If what you say is true, how come I'm always tryin' to figure out why somebody did somethin'? What the hell's it mean? I'm never satisfied with what somethin' just is. I wanna know how come it got that way, or what's gonna happen next because it got that way."

"You're asking me?"

"He sure ain't askin' me."

"Well, the most obvious answer is you're asking the wrong people."

"The fuck I am. I'm askin' exactly the right people. Knowin' somebody did somethin' was never enough. It's never enough. I wanna know why."

"Mario, it's time for you to go home. You're startin' to ask silly questions."

"The hell if I am," Balzic growled, slapping the bar. "Nothin' silly about askin' why."

"Okay," Valcanas said, motioning for Vinnie to fill a glass with cold water and put it in front of Balzic. "You're asking the wrong person because you know very well that neither side in a criminal trial is concerned with the why of anything. And you know that as well as I do."

"That's the fucking court. Trial. Just the facts of the case. Who did what to when. Blah blah blah. Ain't good enough."

"Who did what to whom."

"And how and why? That's what I'm askin' ya. Hows come I gotta bust my brain with that? Nobody else gives a shit."

"He's too low to bail out now," Vinnie said. "He's goin' down in flames."

"Just keep the cold water coming."

"C'mon, Greek, you know the goddamn treeks. Tell me hows come."

"Drink the water. Go 'head."

Balzic drank and held the glass away from him and scowled at it. "I don't want fuckin' water. Zis water? What the hell'm I drinkin' water for? Whatta I look like, a fuckin' octopus?"

"Where's your car?"

"Fuck my car. Where's my why? I don't need my car, I need my why. You gonna help me find it or not?"

"I'll help you find your car, c'mon."

"I don't want my car. I want my why."

Valcanas sighed. "What you want is me to tell you why your mother died, and you're askin' the wrong guy. I have no answer for that."

"Why not? Why don't you pump sunshine up my enemy, gimme a little dupa delight. Pump it right up there, go 'head, I can take it."

"Sunshine what?" Vinnie said, squinting hard at Balzic.

"Sunshine enemies, sunshine enemies, you heard me. Dupa delights."

"What the hell's he talkin' about?"

"I think he means sunshine enemas."

"Right. Yeah. Sunshine enemies. Pump it right up there."

"You want us to pump sunshine up your ass? Is that what you want?"

"No," Balzic said, his head weaving. "'At's zactly what I don't want. Sunshine enemies. They kill ya, all that bullshit ya tell yourself. You got everything figured out . . . ain't got nothin' figured out . . . never figured nothin' out my whole fuckin' life . . . chief of sunshine, 'at's me. . . ."

They got him out to his cruiser, got the keys out of his pants pocket, and Valcanas drove him home while Vinnie followed in his car.

Going up the steps, with Valcanas on one side and Vinnie on the other, Balzic suddenly began to sing. "You are my sunshine . . . my only sunshine . . . you make me happy when skies are gray . . . you'll never know, dear, jus' how I love you . . . please don't take my sunshine away. . . ."

Ruth came to the door, after one of the ladies from the church had opened it. Ruth just shook her head. "Marie, Emily," she called out over her shoulder, "come and help me. I guess he didn't eat anything, did he?"

"Just drank," Valcanas said.

"How 'bout you two? You had anything to eat? Come on and eat, God knows we'll never eat it all—Marie! Emily! C'mere will you please?"

"Why don't we just take him in?" Vinnie said. "If we're comin' in anyway, why not?"

Ruth shrugged. "Come ahead. God, I don't think I've ever seen him this drunk. Hope he doesn't get sick."

"Sick? Sick?" Balzic blustered. "What the hell I get sick for? My sunshine's gone . . . my momma's dead . . . got enemies . . . I'm naked . . . out there by myself . . . I didn't even get a chance to say bye. . . . Hey, Ruth, why'd Marie dye her goddamn hair . . . d'you see her? Huh?" Balzic was weaving largely. Each direction he swayed brought many hands up.

"Go to bed, Mar," Ruth said.

"Sheeeesh. Bed's just goin' spin . . . ask Mo, he knows . . . goddamn bed just spins and spins . . . hate that." He made a serious effort to stand tall. He drew several deep breaths and squared his shoulders. He put his hands on Ruth's shoulders and tried to kiss her on the mouth. He missed by three inches and staggered backward two half-steps. "Don't be pissed at me, 'kay? 'Cause I'm blasted. All these women whisperin' . . . made me nutso . . . don't be pissed, 'kay? You love her more'n me . . . I need her more'n you. See? Scared death . . .

117

scareda death . . . to death, scared to death adeath, see? Nobody get me, see? Now . . . everybody get me . . . all my goddamn enemies . . . I'm out there in the sunshine . . . gotta go beddy-bye. 'Night. . . ."

He lurched around Ruth and stomped and shuffled his way out of the living room with Valcanas and Vinnie close behind, pushing and tugging him away from furniture and walls. They steered him into a bedroom—neither was sure of where Ruth had said to aim him—and got him stretched out on a bed and out of his raincoat and shoes. He was snoring mightily before Valcanas could undo his tie and collar button.

"Holy hell," Vinnie said. "He gets any louder, he's gonna shatter the plaster. Whatta you lookin' for?"

"A wastebasket."

"Good luck. I'm goin' get something to eat."

Valcanas found a metal wastebasket with flowers painted on it and put it beside the bed. Then he followed Vinnie out to the kitchen in search of food, smiling his best lawyery smile at all the women along the way.

*　*　*　*　*

Someone was twisting Balzic gently from side to side, saying, "Daddy, Daddy," and everything was black except for a rectangle of light coming from somewhere beyond his left foot. The light fell across the jaw, neck, and hair of the person prodding him. The twisting and prodding went on for a long time, but eventually it came to him that it was no dream, that it was Marie, and not only was she shaking him to wake him but she was shaking herself, trembling as though from the cold even though she was wrapped in a heavy chamois cloth robe.

"What's the matter? Marie? You okay?"

"No. I didn't mean to startle you. I want to talk to you. But I'm not okay. I mean I am but I'm not, okay?"

"God, Marie," Balzic said, shrugging himself up onto his elbows, "my brain's full of cotton balls—and every one of 'em's soaked with wine. What's the matter? Whatta you wanna talk about?"

"Uh . . . d'you believe in reincarnation?"

"Do I believe in *what*?"

"What happens to us when we die? What do you believe in?"

Balzic squeezed his eyes shut twice. Each time he popped them open, he tried to focus on his daughter's face, but his eyes darted upward to her hair. "I believe you shouldn't've dyed your hair. What the hell d'you do that for?"

"Daddy, I'm serious."

"You think I'm not? Jesus, your hair was beautiful. It was like black olives."

"Could we not talk about hair? Especially mine? I want to know what you believe. Tell me."

"I believe your hair was beautiful just the way it was—"

"Oh shit, Daddy."

"Shit? Did you say *shit*? Since when did you start to use that kind of language?"

"Daddy, I've heard you say everything everybody in the world says plus stuff nobody else would ever think of, and now you're hyper 'cause I said *shit*?"

"Will you stop sayin' that?" he said, squirming away from her until he had his back against the headboard.

"Why? Why should I stop saying that? You say it all the time. You've said it all the time as long as I can remember."

"That's different. That's me."

"What's different about it? It's the same word whether I say it or you say it. Shit is shit."

"No no no no, shit is not—stop that. When I say that, that's different, that's me swearin'. I'm a guy. You're—"

"Oh, Daddy, for god's sake, are you going to give me some male chauvinist propaganda? From you? To me? I can't believe this."

"Propaganda! Little girl, who exactly do you think you're talking to here?"

"Who? You tell me."

"This is—I'm your father."

"So?"

"Whatta you mean, so? What the hell's that mean?"

"Daddy, can we change the subject, please? I really need to know what you think? About death, about whether—what happens to us when we die?"

"Marie, I don't know what time it is, but those cotton balls inside my head just turned to bowling balls and you're askin' me things I couldn't answer if it was the middle of the afternoon and—"

"We never talked about this, Daddy. Never. And I always wanted to ask you about it and now I really have to know. Tonight I really have to know."

"Look, kiddo, I'm no philosopher. I'm a cop. I go to church twice a year, Christmas and Easter, whether I need to or not. One of the people I know best is a priest. But I don't even talk to him about this stuff."

"Why not?"

"You want the truth?"

"Do you think I want you to lie?"

He cleared his throat. His head was pounding, his eyes burning. "Okay. I don't know about any of this stuff. It's way, way over my head. I used to think about it a lot, but it was easy to think about when I was just cruisin' along. Then. . . ."

"Then what?"

"Then I guess I, uh, I found myself in World War II and I wasn't cruisin' anymore. It was like I was in a car goin' a hundred miles an hour and nobody was driving. I was goin' like crazy and I didn't know where."

"So what did you—I mean, did you change how you thought or what you thought about? What did you think about before?"

"I don't know what I thought about before. I guess I was a good little Catholic boy and I guess I thought pretty much what all good little Catholic boys thought."

"And what did you think about after? After you were in the war? Didn't what you thought before, didn't that help?"

"It wasn't a question of helpin'. It just didn't apply. The worst was on an island called Iwo Jima. Some guy said to me one time that his idea of hell was any big city during the rush hour, like being trapped forever on the Parkway East at five o'clock. And I told him my idea of hell was being caught on the beach on Iwo Jima while the Japs were still up on Mount Suribachi. Lotsa people say there are no atheists in foxholes—you know what a foxhole is?"

"Yeah. It's a hole you dig for protection, isn't it?"

"That's close enough. But I remember thinkin'—I remember this very clearly—if there was a god and he was standin' by and watchin' that happen, what was goin' on there, and didn't stop it, then either he wasn't really as powerful as he was made out to be, or else if he was, then he sure wasn't anybody I was ever gonna pray to, because I saw a kind of pain there I still can't believe. What I'm tryin' to say, and I don't know if this makes any sense to you, but the only way I could get through that was by tellin' myself that it was hell. I mean, I told myself, *this is hell* . . . noise you can't believe. The smell of that black ash from the volcano, the smell of gunpowder, the smell of . . . everything else . . . the screamin' . . . it was only by tellin' myself that there was nothing worse or could ever be anything worse, that was the only way I got through it 'cause no matter what you did, there was nothing you could do to protect yourself . . . which is pretty much the way I feel now. Naked. And yet you know you have to get up and move on. . . . To answer your question, I have no idea what I think about reincarnation, except . . . if I lived before I have no memory of it."

"Don't you think about it any other way?"

Balzic shook his head.

"But what about Grandma? What do you think is going to happen to her?"

"I just told you: This stuff's way over my head. I can't pretend to talk about it intelligently. I only know what I know. Which isn't much."

"Did you ever talk about it with her? Do you know what she believed?"

"Uh, we tried to talk about it once, right after I got discharged. I don't know what brought it up—I guess probably I wasn't goin' to church often enough. I'm not sure how we got started on it, but I remember we had a really bad fight about it. She stayed mad at me for a long time."

"But what did she believe—did she say?"

"I really don't remember, Marie. I guess she must've believed what all Catholics are supposed to believe about it. If she didn't, I can't imagine what we would've been arguin' about."

121

"So . . . so in all the time you sent Em and me to church, you never believed any of it?"

"In the first place, *I* didn't send you. You went with your mother and grandmother."

"You never believed any of it? Nothing at all?"

Balzic sighed heavily, but said nothing.

"Aren't you going to tell me—this is pretty important."

"I guess you wouldn't be wakin' me up in the middle of the night if you didn't think it was."

"Well?"

"It's not easy to answer you, you know."

"Why not? All you have to do is be honest. What's hard about that?"

Balzic snorted. "It's not as easy bein' honest at my age as it is at yours."

"I can't believe you said that, Daddy. I mean, shit, that's really some statement to be makin' to me—"

"Will you stop usin' that language!"

"Can we just skip the language? Why's it so hard to be honest at your age? Harder than it is at mine? I don't get that at all."

"'Cause at your age—well, things are a lot less complicated."

"Whaaaaat?"

"I mean that at my age things are a lot more complicated. You—not you, me—I just see that things go off in a lot more different directions than they did when I was younger."

"You're losing me, Daddy, you'd better—"

"Okay okay. What I mean is, lemme tell you about what I said before, about havin' this terrible fight with Ma after I got discharged from the Marine Corps. See, when I was that age, what I believed in was honesty. So I told her what I believed in or what I didn't believe in, and it hurt her, real bad. See, if that situation had come up now, I would've never argued with her about it. I would've just dummied up, because it would've been more important to me to not cause her any grief than it would've been to be honest and tell her the truth. 'Cause it wouldn't have hurt me to go along with her. I could've gone to church, could've gone through the motions, I could've found somethin' to think about while I was there."

"But you would have been a phony. And I can't see you as a phony. I've never, ever thought of you as a phony."

"So what?"

"What do you mean, so what? I pay you a compliment and you say, 'So what?' And in so many words you tell me you'd rather be a phony? So—so much for my compliment, I guess."

"Well, see that's what I meant about it bein' more complicated when you're older. I think."

"Jesus, Daddy, what you're saying is, you don't believe in anything about what happens after we die and it's better not to talk about it. That's pretty shitty, if you want to know." Her chin sank and then it started to quiver and she began to sob, quietly.

"Look, little one, I'm sorry I don't know what you want me to know—"

"I don't want you to *know* anything. I want you to tell me what you *believe*. Why can't you do that?"

"That's easy. I don't know what I believe. I don't think about it. 'Cause every time I do it scares me. And I guess that's what's left over from bein' a good little Catholic boy. I still carry the bags: if I do wrong, then when I die I'm gonna burn in hell."

"Even though you don't believe it?"

"Lemme tell ya about a guy I know. He's Russian. His parents came from the old country. I don't know if his mother did, but his father did and her parents did, that I know. Now I don't know whether this is a Russian belief or maybe just his family believed it, but when he was a little kid, every time there was an electrical storm, his family told him that was God makin' all that fire and noise 'cause he was mad because little boys didn't do what they were told, didn't listen to their parents or their grandparents or their teachers. So anyway, when he grew up, you know what he thinks religion is? He thinks it's just another way rich people keep poor people in line, give 'em a lotta rules just to keep 'em workin', payin' taxes, and not killin' anybody unless there's a war. He can talk on this subject for hours and hours. I've heard him. But can you guess what happens to him when there's a thunderstorm? Huh?"

"He becomes a little boy again?"

"Right. Only way he can get through a storm is by drinkin'—

down in his cellar. He admits it. Storms just scare the hell out of him 'cause he just knows he's been a bad boy."

"I suppose that's a real good story, Daddy, but it doesn't tell me about you. It—"

"Of course it does. It's just a different say of sayin' what I've already told you about me. I try not to think about anything that happens when you die because I become a little boy again. A bad little boy, and I know I've broken all the rules."

"You? You broke all the rules? My god, you *are* the rules."

Balzic snorted and shook his head. "God, Marie, you're young. Listen, how 'bout lettin' me go back to sleep, okay? Tomorrow's gonna be one hell of a day, and it's comin' a hundred miles an hour. I don't want to see what I know I have to look at today. I'm sorry I haven't been more help to you, but you really gotta let me get some more sleep, or I'm gonna come apart at the seams, okay?"

"Okay," she said. She leaned forward and kissed him on the cheek. He patted her hand. Then she was gone and so was the rectangle of light after she closed the door.

*   *   *   *   *

At half-past noon, Balzic led his wife and daughters into the front parlor of Sal Bruno's Funeral Home. Balzic had tried to steel himself for this moment with two cups of black coffee laced with Sambuca, but it wasn't enough. The moment he saw his mother in her coffin, his knees went soft, the acid gurgled up in the back of his throat, and everything he looked at started to shimmer as though he were standing on a long, flat road in August on an afternoon when there were no clouds. He quickened his pace, not to leave his family behind, but to get to the padded bar in front of the coffin so he could kneel and support himself on the elbow rest. He tried to tell himself that he had to be strong for his family, but by the time he was kneeling and crossing himself and examining his mother's face for signs of life, he had forgotten his family and was sobbing uncontrollably. All he could see, all he could think of, was that his mother looked like every other corpse he'd ever seen in funeral homes and he wanted her, with everything that was in him, to not look like them.

"What the hell's she wearin' glasses for?" he blurted out. He sounded like he was shouting, but that was only because there were so few other sounds.

"Mario!" Ruth tried to whisper.

"Well what the hell's she gonna be lookin' at? Huh? I'm takin' them off." He heaved himself up, and got instantly lightheaded and nearly fell into a huge basket of lilies from the FOP.

"Mario, let me do it, okay? Just try to calm down, okay?"

"I don't wanna calm down. I get any calmer I'm gonna pass out. You want to take her glasses off, go ahead. I'm not gonna fight you for it. Just so somebody takes 'em off. Looks grotesque for crissake."

"Please try to not talk so loud, Mar, okay?" Ruth said, sidling around him and reaching into the coffin to remove the glasses. "What should I do with them?"

"Leave 'em in there. Just put 'em on the side. You want 'em? I don't want 'em. Where'd they get that dress?"

"We brought it last night."

"Who, we? You and me, that we? I don't remember that."

"Marie and Emily and me, that we. Not you. You were out."

"You mean out of the house or passed out?"

"Passed out." Ruth nudged him on the shoulder. "Blow your nose, Mar."

"Huh? Oh. Yeah."

"What do we do now?" Emily said.

"We be nice to the people who come, that's what we do," Marie said.

"Be nice? Like how? What do you say?"

"They're going to say they're sorry and how nice she looks and how much they liked her and how much they're going to miss her and you're going to thank them, that's what you say. It's not hard, just do what you think you ought to, you won't be wrong." Ruth licked her fingers and tried to put down an unruly curl above Emily's ear. "You'll be okay."

Balzic couldn't take his eyes off his mother's face. He reached out and patted her hands and almost recoiled from their coldness and hardness. "Jesus," he said to himself, "I gotta sit down."

"What did you say, Mar?"

"I said I gotta sit down. These damn flowers are makin' me sick, don't they make you sick?" He turned away from the coffin and walked stiffly to a chair on the side of the room where there were only two or three baskets of flowers, and he sank into it. Just as he did, a deliveryman from a florist carried in two wreaths, each of them a yard across, and propped them up in a corner of the room opposite from Balzic.

People began to come in, mostly women, and mostly Balzic stood up and shook hands with some and embraced others and said thanks a lot. It was all fuzzy around the edges, faces, voices, words. Some women were crying softly, one or two were making a lot of noise; the smell of lilies and roses was so strong it seemed to Balzic to mix with the sounds like a thick liquid that oozed everywhere and made the simplest movements next to impossible.

Every so often, he felt someone putting an arm around his waist and he would look down and it would be Emily, who seemed to be taking this harder than anybody, except she wasn't saying anything. Her eyes were puffy and raw and she looked small and lonely. Balzic would squeeze her shoulders and for a moment it would seem to help; then she'd drift away and stand by herself, staring at the coffin and chewing the inside of her lower lip.

"Mario . . . Mario," someone was saying sharply into his ear.

"Huh? What?"

It was Sal Bruno. "There's a guy outside says he has to see you. Says it's very urgent. He's in the parking lot."

Balzic was befuddled. "Wants to see me?"

"Yes. I told him your mother was here. He said he didn't care, he had to talk to you now. Absolutely. Uh, this is none of my business, but this guy did not look all right, if you know what I mean. Maybe you want me to call your station? What do you think?"

"Why'd you put my mother's glasses on, Sallie? I don't understand that. Do some people want that?"

Bruno cleared his throat. "Uh, yes, some people think it looks more natural. Maybe I should call your station. I'm going to do that, is that all right with you?"

"No it's not all right with me. Where is this guy? In the parking lot?" They started walking to the front door. "Some people actually think it looks more natural, is that what you said? You know what, Sallie? Those people are stupid."

Bruno shrugged. "I didn't say I approved or disapproved. If there's a fault here, it's that I didn't ask you—"

"Never mind. Took 'em off anyway." Balzic was out and bounding down the walk toward the parking lot. At the end of the walk was a tall man in a dark blue jacket and pants with his back to the wind, smoking and watching Balzic. His shoes were greasy and the heels were run down.

He flipped the cigarette away as Balzic approached and said, "You the cop? The chief?"

Balzic nodded and stopped two steps away. "I'm the chief of police in Rocksburg, yes. You wanna see me?"

"Leave my wife the fuck alone, you hear me?"

"What? What're you talkin' about?"

"Hey, clean the shit outta your ears. You heard what I said. You want me to say it louder? Listen up. Leave my wife the fuck alone."

"Since you haven't told me what your name is, I don't know who your wife is—and let's go over here away from the walk here. And tone your language down. There's a lot of women goin' in and out here who don't like that kind of language—"

"Hey fuck them huh? I ain't goin' nowhere. And I'm not gonna tell you again—stay the fuck away from my wife." He was almost shouting.

Several women, in groups of twos and threes, recoiled and hurried around them.

"Tone it down, you hear? You're startin' to embarrass me. These ladies could take what you're sayin' the wrong way, understand?"

"That's your problem. You look like you're worried what women think. You'd be a lot fuckin' better off if you started worryin' what I think, which is, leave my wife the fuck alone."

"You have a name?"

127

The loud man paused for a long moment and then started to laugh and walk away, backwards. "You really don't know what my name is, do you? That's funny." He laughed very hard and was still laughing when he got into a dirty red Chevy pickup truck with a green fender and a blue door on the right side and drove out of the lot. He was still laughing as he looked through the rear window at Balzic. Balzic waited until the truck was out of sight before he took out his notebook and pen and wrote down the license number.

Back inside the funeral home, he found Sal Bruno and asked to use his office phone. Bruno took him to it, on the second floor, and left him alone.

Balzic called his station, and Sergeant Joe Royer answered. "Mario, I want you to know both me and the wife are real sorry about your mother and if there's anything we can do, just say it."

"Thank you, Joe. I appreciate it. Right now, how 'bout runnin' this license number through, okay?"

After Royer had taken the number, he said, "Then what?"

"Well, first I want his name and address. Then priors and outstandings, you know, everything. Here's the phone number here. I'll be waitin' here."

Royer called back six minutes later. "This is a busy man."

"Yeah? How busy?"

"Two suspensions. One for fifteen days in 1984 for doin' eighty-five in a thirty-five zone; one for thirty days in 1987, DUI. Also, he's got several priors: assault, reckless endangerment, prohibited offensive weapon—twice on all of those—plus one harassment by communications. Did no time for any of the preceding, but he did do eleven months for another harassment by communications, terroristic threats, and intimidation of witness. Complainant was his mother. Real sweetheart, this guy. Name's Hryczk, Richard Joseph. H-R-Y-C-Z-K. Box 105 Elderton Road, Rocksburg, RD3. That's out in Westfield Township. I know right where it is. I used to go with a girl lived on that road right after I got out of the army. So what do you wanna do with this guy?"

"I wanna find out if he has a son. Call the house. Ask to talk to the son. Make up something about sellin' a car, you know, or buyin' one, or buyin' some parts. I want to know if he has a son."

"And if he does, then what?"

"Just find that out first. And call me right back. I'll still be here."

A few minutes later, Royer called back. "He's got a son. John. Very nervous about something. Wanted to know how I got his phone number. Didn't sound like he believed anything I told him. So now what?"

"So nothing for now. I don't know. Thanks. I'll see you."

Balzic thought for a minute, then picked up the phone again and dialed the state-police barracks.

When the dispatcher answered, Balzic identified himself and asked to speak to Trooper Schieb.

"Trooper Schieb, may I help you?"

"This is Balzic. Chief of Rocksburg PD."

"Oh yeah. I was wondering when I was gonna hear from you. What's up?"

"Well, you tell me. Whatta you have on the body behind the bookstore?"

"We got a sudden burst of cooperation from the clerk. Gave us a good mug from the Ident-i-Kit. Caucasian, tall, slender, early twenties, had a folding knife in a leather sheath with a snap cover. Clerk said he went outside with the victim after the victim asked him if he wanted to smoke some weed. The clerk says he did not see any vehicles, didn't hear any noise, and never saw either one of them again. He had, however, seen the victim many times before; made him for a fag hustlin' the truckers. Also, he said he'd seen the guy with the knife once or twice before but never paid any attention to him. The guy came in, pumped his money into the peep shows, and left. And that's about where I am. So where are you?"

"Where I am, I think, is on a line to your tall, slender Caucasian in his early twenties. I'm not bettin' anything on this just yet, but I think you ought to go take a look at this guy."

"Wait a sec till I get my pen. I dropped it. Okay, go."

"John Hryczk. H-R-Y-C-Z-K. Box 105 Elderton Road, Rocksburg, RD3. I don't know where that is, but my deskman told me he knows exactly where it is."

"So do I. I've busted the, uh, I guess it was this guy's old man once. Richard. And I think it was, lemme think, yeah, Ralph Hurley busted him too."

"What for?"

"I got him on a DUI. He was drivin' through people's yards out there. Hurley got him for aggravated assault. He was tryin' to hang his wife from a tree, except he was so drunk he had the rope around her neck and under one armpit or he probably would've killed her, 'cause Hurley told me when he got there the woman's feet were off the ground. Naturally she was too scared to prosecute and that was before we got the word we were supposed to make the bust on our own. Which is neither here nor there. How'd you connect the son to this? What's the connection?"

"I don't think I'll tell you that just yet. I think you should go out there and get a look at him and see if you can make him from the Ident-i-Kit mug."

"Oh come on, man, you have to do better than that. There's nobody here except the dispatcher and a lab guy, and I'm not goin' out there by myself. That clown has at least one shotgun, if I remember it right, and he has a history of heavy violence. I'm not goin' to go knock on his door by myself and say, Hey, I came to get a peek at your son, you wanna trot him out for me? No, thanks. I've been doin' this gig just long enough to know that there's nothing sadistic drunks like doin' more than showin' off for their male children. Unless you want to go along? What do you say? You can carry the mug shot, I'll carry the shotgun. Or you can carry the shotgun, I'm flexible."

"Uh, I'm in a funeral home. My mother's here."

"Oh. Well. I'm sorry. You have my sympathy. So, uh, I'll just wait till I get some backup before I go check out the son."

"Hey, whatever makes you comfortable."

"Well, in the meantime, I'll keep you up, okay? And I really am sorry about your mother. I hope she didn't suffer."

"Thank you. I don't know whether she did or not. Just one more thing; the mother's the one who wants to tell me about this, but she's scared out of her mind. I suspected why, but now I know from what you told me. I gotta go. I gotta go talk to the people."

*   *   *   *   *

At four-thirty in the afternoon, as they were getting ready to go home to get something to eat, Sal Bruno told Balzic there was a phone call for him. Balzic took the call in Bruno's office.

"Mario? This is Fischetti. I'm real sorry to bother you about this now—you have my sympathy. I'm real sorry about your mom."

"Thank you, Larry."

"So, uh, I really don't want to bother you—now, I mean—but I got a bad one here. Real real bad A and B. I mean this woman is a mess. Her face looks like a red potato. Neighbor called it in to the state police and they didn't have anybody available, so they asked us to go out. So all I did was when I got there I just called the ambulance. There was nobody there, the woman was on the front porch. Tell you the truth, I thought she was dead, there was blood everywhere."

"So what's the problem?"

"Well, I don't know how to handle it. How do I write it up?"

"Just fill out a special-incident report, just the way it happened. What are you worried about?"

"I'm not worried, I just never did this before. Every time I ever went out in the townships before, I was just backin' 'em up. I never had to do the paper. Man, I don't think this woman's gonna make it. I've seen a ton of hurtin' put on people, but I've never seen anything like this before. Her nose is bent over so far, one nostril is completely closed. Okay, so I'll see you tonight probably."

"Wait a second. What township?"

"Westfield?"

"Where? This wasn't on Elderton Road by any chance?"

"Yeah. Uh, Box 105."

"Jeez-sus. Hryczk, is that it?"

"Yeah. That's what her operator's license says."

"Sonofabitch came here about two hours ago and threatened me to stay away from her."

"Threatened *you*?"

"Yeah. She tried to talk to me twice. She thought her son did something, but she couldn't tell me. Just kept fishin' for what could happen. Then her old man threatens me and she winds up where you are. So anyway, call Schieb at Troop A. Tell him what happened—if you haven't already."

"No no, I just got back. You're the first call I made."

"Well, call him and you work it out with him, okay? Just make sure you cover your ass. I'm not jokin'—there's at least one loony, maybe two in that house. Schieb busted the guy once, and he wouldn't go out alone—Schieb, I mean. I'm goin' home now. I'll probably be there until quarter to seven, then I'll be back here until nine, nine-thirty."

"Okay, Mario. I'll be careful. I will. And I'll call you."

Sal Bruno was waiting outside his office. "Anything I can do, Mario?"

"Nah, nothing. Listen, I may say a lot of things here over the next couple of days. Don't take any of it personally, okay? I'm just so goddamned rattled I don't know half what I'm doin' and only a little bit of what I'm sayin', understand?"

Bruno nodded and shrugged. "You don't have to say any—"

"I want to, Sal. I want you to know I appreciate what you've done—what you're doin'. I'll never forget it. So no matter what I may say, like about her glasses, that doesn't change anything. I'm just rattled, just runnin' my mouth. Most of the time I don't realize what I say—I mean how I say what I say affects people, you know? Like last night—you wanna hear this? You don't wanna hear this."

"No. Of course I do. Say it, tell me."

"Yeah? You really wanna hear it? Well, last night, in the middle of the night my oldest girl wakes me up, she wants to know what I think about what happens after we die, and in the course of the conversation she says *shit*. And *shitty*. And I'll tell ya, Sal, I was shocked and she never batted an eye and when I said something about it, she says I say stuff like that all the time and if it's okay for me to say stuff like that, it's okay for her to say it—hey, why don't we walk to the car while I'm tellin' you this, they're gonna wonder what happened to me. You sure you wanna hear this?"

"Of course, of course."

"Yeah, well, okay, see I had no idea my daughter's been listen' to me all these years and I mean she is a grown woman, she's not a little girl anymore, but still when she used that kind of language, it shocked me, it really did. Especially when she told me it was because, in so many words, I talked like that. So I didn't understand how I was influencin' her in a bad way, if you know what I mean. So I'm thinkin', is she a worse person because of that? Or should I be flattered 'cause she sort of tries to be like me—in maybe just this way—"

"Mario! Come on, what are you doing?" Ruth shouted at him from inside the car.

"Aw fuck, I gotta go, Sallie. I'll talk to you some other time maybe, okay? And I really appreciate what you're doin'. I'll see you later."

Balzic lumbered over to the car and got in, mumbling a half-hearted apology for keeping everybody waiting.

Back home, in the kitchen, Ruth leaned close to Balzic and said, "You can't let it alone even when your mother's . . . you can't let it alone, can you?"

"Let what alone? What're you talkin' about?"

"You're forever a cop. Always, always and forever. You're not capable of taking a break. I always told myself I knew that, but I never knew how much you're not able to take a break until today."

"I don't know what you're talkin' about, Ruth, but your tone is not real friendly. If you're talkin' about me makin' phone calls out of Sal Bruno's office, yeah, I was—"

"I don't need you to confess—"

"Than what the hell do you need?"

"I really have to say it, don't I? I mean, you really don't know?"

"For crissake, Ruth, just say it, will you? I hate these conversations where I'm catchin' flak 'cause I don't know something I'm supposed to know and it's obvious to everyone in the whole world except me what it is I don't know. Just tell me, okay?"

"I—I need you. My best friend is gone and I need you and I don't need you to be a cop. Everybody in America gets three days off for a death in the immediate family. Take the goddamn three days off. Give them to me! Give me you. All of you. Not just the you between that goddamned woman and those goddamned phone calls. Not just when you can squeeze me in.

We spent two and a half hours in the funeral home, Mario. You never touched me. You never came near me again after I took her glasses off. And if that wasn't enough, you were on the phone or outside for almost forty minutes. Jesus Christ, Mario, I looked at you today once and—I must've stared at you for a minute and you looked right through me. You're doing it now. You're lookin' right through me again. It's like you wish I wasn't here. Is that what you wish?"

"You're not makin' any sense. I'm lookin' at you, I'm not staring through you."

"God, Mario, you look mad enough to hit me."

"Oh stop it for crissake. You really are comin' off the wall now."

"Will you listen to how you're talking to me? Will you just listen?"

Balzic blew out a heavy breath. "Look, I'm tired, I'm hungry, I'm thirsty—"

"You think I'm not? You think you're the only one?"

Balzic glared at her. "You think maybe we could, uh, declare an armistice? A ceasefire? You know, for the duration? You think maybe we could do that?"

"No," she said.

"Oh shit. Why not?"

"Because we need to think about something. I've been thinking about it the whole two and a half hours we were there."

"Think about what?"

"The reason we're so snotty to each other."

"I'm listenin'," he said.

"This isn't going to be easy to say, so you have to promise to not interrupt me. 'Cause I really don't know how to say it. I just know I have to say it."

Balzic held up his hands, palms up. "So? Say it."

"Okay. We used her. Both of us. We used her to make the marriage. She was—she was almost like my substitute husband. Not almost. She was. That's exactly what she was. It's how I managed to live with you all the times you were gone. I said, that's okay, go, I always have your mother. I didn't have you, I had your mother. Fine. And it got to the point where I didn't even miss you anymore. It got to that point a long time ago.

"Only now, she's not here for me to use like that anymore. And you're gone the way you always are. You haven't changed. But now I'm going to have to change. And I'm scared. 'Cause you and me have never been alone . . . together. Do you know that? Did you ever think about it? Doesn't it scare you?"

"Is it okay for me to talk now?"

"Yeah. I'm done. Go 'head and talk."

"Exactly how—you said how you used her. Exactly how did I use her?"

"The same way! You knew you could go and you could stay gone 'cause you knew she'd be here. You used her to be you. That's how we worked this marriage. And now we have to learn a whole new way. And it scares me to death."

"You sound like this was something I sat down and planned out. Like I schemed it out."

"No no. I didn't say that. I'm not saying you did that. Me either. We just sort of, I don't know, backed into it. And it worked. And fortunately for me, I really loved her and liked her and she was real easy to get along with. She was the best. But I knew today how much I missed her. I mean I found out. Mario, we're startin' all over again. And you're not the only one out there naked in the sunshine. You're not. . . ."

Balzic pulled open the fridge and bent down to peer in. "Where's the wine? This thing's so fulla stuff I can't find anything."

"It's probably where it always is. Who would move it? It probably just got pushed back a little bit."

"It's not here, I'm tellin' ya."

"Let me see." She bent around him and started moving bowls and cartons and containers. "What's this?" she said, straightening up and holding the carafe out to him.

"Couldn't see it," he muttered. "Like I suppose I can't see some other things around here."

"Mario, honest to god—don't you think it's time both of us quit feeling so goddamned sorry for ourselves? Huh? Don't you think it's time? I mean I understand mourning. I understand grief. We're entitled to that. That's okay. But we've got to stop this—this being so goddamned defensive. Really. Instead of just feeling like I attacked you 'cause I said what I said, would you just please *think* about what I said instead of feeling attacked? Believe me, I'm more scared about what I said—I mean I feel like we used your mother to not grow up! She was our parent, our mother, father, husband. Jesus, you can't believe I feel good about that. Can you?"

Balzic was still holding the carafe in both hands. He got a wine glass from a cabinet and filled it two-thirds full.

"I don't know what I believe about that. I always thought—I mean I think I thought it, I don't recall talkin' to anybody about it, but I think I thought I was being a good son by havin' her live with us. I mean where the hell was she gonna go? It never occurred to me for her to be someplace else. She was supposed to be here. I wasn't usin' her to keep from growin' up."

"Mario, I said we backed into it. It wasn't something we did on purpose. It just all worked out that way, but that workin' out, that kept us from dealing with what we're going to have to deal with now. Do you see what I'm saying?"

He took a long drink of wine, two large swallows, and said, "Does this mean you're scared—when you find out it's just you and me now—you're gonna discover I'm the world's biggest asshole and you're wonderin' why the hell you ever married me?"

She shrugged and grimaced and rolled her eyes. "That's a hell of a way to put it, but I guess I'm scared for both of us. I'm scared you're going to look at me one night and say, 'God, do you have anything intelligent to talk about?' How 'bout pourin' me a glass of that? Where'd the girls get to?"

"I thought they went upstairs. Why? They don't live here anymore either, you know. You wanna bring 'em down so we can bounce off them or what?"

"No. I was thinking maybe we could get them to fix us something to eat. I'm so tired I could go to sleep standing up."

"Here," he said, handing her a glass of wine. "I'll see what I can con 'em into."

"Don't con. Just ask."

He started through the living room, but the phone's ringing

stopped him. He picked it up without turning to look at his wife.

"It's Fischetti, Mario."

"Yeah. So what's up?"

"I really hate to do this to you, but . . ."

"Just tell me, okay?"

"I think you should come up here. The woman? The one all beat up?"

"Yeah."

"Her son's here. He wants to talk to you. Says he won't talk to anybody else, and he says you better hurry up before his father gets here."

"Ah shit." Balzic rubbed his forehead and temples. "Okay. I'll be there in a couple minutes. You still in—where are you?"

"Emergency, uh, trauma unit."

"Okay. I'll find you." He hung up and turned to look at Ruth, who was fuming.

"Don't say a word," she said. "Just go."

"I'll see you at seven o'clock, okay? I'll be there. I will."

"Just go."

*   *   *   *   *

Once in the trauma unit of Conemaugh General Hospital, Balzic went peeking into treatment rooms until he found Fischetti talking quietly with a nurse in the last treatment room on the right side of the corridor.

Fischetti excused himself from the nurse and stepped out into the hall. He motioned with his index finger toward the room behind Balzic. "In there. The docs are gettin' ready to put her on a respirator."

"Where's the kid?"

"He was in the john throwin' up a minute ago. Should be comin' out soon."

"When'd he come in?"

"Wasn't very long after I talked to you when you were in Bruno's. He just came in and tried to talk to her a couple of times. I hung around until he went out for a smoke. Then he approached me when I was thinkin' about goin' up to him. He

137

asked me what your name was and would I call you. I told him and then I wasted a lot of time tryin' to get him to tell me what he knew about what happened to his mother."

"What'd he tell you?"

"Nothing. But he got the fidgets more and more and I started thinkin' maybe he's who worked her over, but then he started talkin' about talkin' to you before his old man got here, and so that's where we are—I think."

"He didn't say anything else?"

"About what?"

"About anything."

Fischetti shook his head no.

"Well, listen, I'm gonna try to talk to him back here—if I can find some room. What I want you to do is go out by the desk, and if a big tall guy in greasy shoes, looks anything like the kid, if he shows up lookin' for his wife, you stop him. Do whatever you have to, except don't shoot him. But use your piece and try to get him cuffed around a pipe—if you can find one. He's got a history of beatin' on people, so watch your ass, you hear me?"

Fischetti nodded.

"No heroics. Starts goin' his way, holler, *cabeesh*?"

"I hear ya."

Fischetti set off for the waiting room, and Balzic turned around just as a tall, long-haired man in his early twenties stepped into the hall.

"I'm Chief of Police Balzic, Rocksburg Police. You lookin' for me?"

"I guess," the young man said, his voice so soft Balzic barely heard him.

"You wanna step over here?" Balzic motioned to the room where he'd first seen Fischetti talking to the nurse.

The young man shrugged and followed Balzic in. He shifted from foot to foot and hooked his thumbs into his jeans pockets, then into his belt, then into his back pockets.

"Guess you ain't allowed to smoke in here, huh?"

"No, you're not. I don't even think you're allowed to do that in the waiting room anymore."

"You wouldn't have any gum on ya, would you?"

"No, I don't."

"My mouth tastes real awful . . . I just was sick couple minutes ago."

"Maybe the next time we see a nurse, maybe she can find you a Tums or Titralac or Rolaids or somethin'."

"Maybe," he said, shrugging several times. He looked at the floor.

"Patrolman Fischetti says you want to talk to me."

"Who?"

"The police officer who was just here—with your mother?"

"Oh. Him. Yeah. I mean yeah I know who he is."

"Uh-ha. So?"

"So what?"

"So do you wanna talk to me?"

He whistled out a breath and shrugged and chewed his lower lip. "I guess."

Balzic waited.

He started to belch and rubbed his fingers hard across his mouth several times. "I'm gonna get sick." He bolted out of the room and down the hall into the public john. Balzic could hear him retching and heaving.

Balzic spotted the nurse Fischetti had been talking to earlier and asked her if she had some antacids or a toothbrush and some toothpaste. "The kid in the john's throwin' up. He could use something that would give him a better taste."

She said she'd see what she could do and disappeared. In a few moments she was back and she held out a sample bottle of Titralac. "These should help," she said, and then she was gone again.

Balzic gave them to John Hryczk when he came back from the john, his eyes red and teary, his face flushed.

"What's this?"

"It's an antacid. Put two or three in your mouth and chew 'em up. Give you a good taste—or better than the one you got."

He fumbled with the lid and then with the foil and the cotton and finally put two of the tablets in his mouth and began tentatively to chew.

"They'll do the trick, believe me."

Hryczk chewed faster and nodded and chewed more and nodded again. "Pretty good."

"So, uh, listen, John—it is John, right?"

"Yeah. Uh-ha."

"Well, John, what is it you wanna talk about?"

He sighed heavily. "Oh God. Everything. I wish I could." He was staring at a point over Balzic's right shoulder. "But I think I really oughta, you know, like have a lawyer here. Only I don't know any lawyers 'cept the ones in the public defender's."

"Been in trouble with the law before, John?"

Hryczk nodded slowly, dropping his gaze to the floor. "Coupla times."

"As a juvenile or adult?"

"Juvee."

"Never as an adult?"

He shook his head no.

"That's all changed now, right?"

"I guess," Hryczk said so low Balzic could barely hear him.

"So, uh, John, you wanna tell me something, or would you feel more comfortable if we went and got you a lawyer? It's up to you. But if you don't wanna wait until we get you a lawyer, you have to know that I really can't talk to you anymore unless you sign a piece of paper that says you give up your right to have an attorney present. Do you understand what I'm sayin' to you?"

"I think, yeah."

"So what's it gonna be, John? You want a lawyer? Or you wanna sign a waiver?"

"I just right now—like for now I wanna say I can't handle this anymore. I mean, what my—what happened to my ma, I can't handle that no more. I can't be . . . I can't do that . . . I mean, I can't just stand around and watch it happen to her no more. And I know my fath—my old man, I can't just sit around and watch her get beat up like this. It makes me sick every time. I can't keep nothin' down. Everything I eat, when this happens, it just comes right up. And I'm so scareda him . . . holy shit, I can't . . . I mean I know he's gonna come up here pretty soon. He'll go home eventually and then he'll see I ain't there and he'll be right up here, and, man, the shit'll hit the fan then."

"Why's that, exactly?"

"'Cause look what he did to her 'cause he found out she was talkin' to you. Same thing'll . . . never mind."

"No, go 'head, say it."

"Can't, man. Can't even . . . I almost can't even think about it."

"You like your mother, John?"

"Nah. No . . . one time she found a dog, it was hit by a car and it had one leg all mangled. She had it in the kitchen. . . . He came home, he saw it, just grabbed it, just picked it up and smashed it into the wall. Then he rubbed it all over her face. . . . Just rubbed the blood all over her face. . . . She wasn't allowed to talk to nothin' 'less she asked him first. . . ."

"If you don't like her, John, why're you here?"

He shrugged. "Don't know. I guess . . . guess it was because she talked to you about me. . . ."

"And she got beat up for that, is that it?"

"I guess."

"Make you feel a little bit responsible, is that what it does?"

"Maybe. I don't know."

"Well let me put it to you this way, John. If it wasn't for you, she never would've come to talk to me. And if she hadn't talked to me, her husband wouldn't have done this to her, is that right?"

"I guess."

"Let me ask you, John, her husband is your father, right? I mean he's not a stepfather, right?"

"Yeah. Right."

"Well, John, I think it's time you made up your mind. Either you waive your right to an attorney, or else we go find you one. Whatta you say?"

Hryczk looked at the floor for a long moment. "I don't want to go away from here right now. I wanna wait till I know how she's doin', okay?"

"Uh, John, I can appreciate it, I can understand it, but see, the thing is, I'm in the middle of something else, and if I don't get back there in time I'm gonna have a real problem. I mean, I know we all have problems, you wanna see how your mother's gonna be, you're worried about your father showin' up. But I got a problem too. My mother's in a funeral home."

"Huh?"

"She died yesterday."

"Oh Jesus shit I'm gonna be sick," he said, whirling away from Balzic and out of the room toward the john again.

Balzic stepped into the hall to see if Hryczk was indeed going to the john. He was.

A ruddy-faced young man in green scrub clothes stepped into the hall from another room and collided with Balzic.

"You in charge?" Balzic said.

"Yes."

Balzic produced his ID. The young man peered at it for a moment, then shrugged. "What's on your mind?"

"Uh, that woman across the hall there?" Balzic pointed at the room he thought Mrs. Hryczk was in. "What's the story with her?"

"Probably gallstones. Maybe an ulcer. Maybe—"

"No no. We're not talkin' about the same woman. I mean the one that's all beat up."

"Oh she's not in that room. The woman you're looking for is in the head-trauma unit."

"Since when?"

"More than an hour ago, I'd say. I'd have to check the log to see when she went up, but it was at least an hour ago."

"Well, uh, so you examined her?"

"Yes."

"What kind of shape's she in?"

"Not very good, I'm afraid."

"How so?"

"Her pictures were not encouraging. She'd taken some terrific blows; I can't say from what. I called a neurosurgeon as soon as I saw her pictures. She had at least three fractures, not including the cartilage in her nose. I would imagine she's in surgery now. I'm guessing, but it's a reasonable guess that there was bleeding in the brain. You could feel the depression above her left eyebrow. Her blood pressure was dropping, she had fewer and fewer moments of lucidity."

"You mean she was awake when she was brought in?"

"When I first saw her, she was, yes."

"She tell you anything?"

"Like what anything? Like who did it?"

"Yeah."

"No. Mostly what she said was her head hurt."

"Never said a word about what happened?"

"Not in my presence." The young doctor shrugged again. "You might ask the nurses. They were with her more than I was. I had several other people to see. 'Course, we were all in and out. We were all pretty busy for an hour there."

"You care to offer an opinion about what caused her problem?"

"Probably her husband—but you know, of course, that I'm not going to testify to that. I have no way of knowing that."

"Yeah, sure, but what did her injuries look like? They look like she was in a car wreck, she look like she fell outta bed, what?"

"Well, to be perfectly honest, you're out of my area of expertise. That's for a forensic pathologist to say, not me. Or at least I think it is."

"Well what did she look like? I mean, did you just start workin' here yesterday?"

"No. No, I didn't. But, look, I don't know you. I don't know what you're going to do with how I answer your questions. For all I know you're wearing a voice-activated tape recorder. Six months from now I could be looking at a subpoena. I prefer not to, if you know what I mean. Working in a trauma unit, I'm already payin' insurance rates that bring tears to my eyes. I don't need to put myself in any more jeopardy."

"Okay. Off the record—and on that you have my promise that I will not come back to haunt you six months from now—just tell me what your best guess is about how the woman got those injuries. Can you do that?"

"Off the record? Your promise, right?"

Balzic nodded.

"Why do you need to ask me this? You know—or you can make as good a guess as I can make—how the woman reached her present condition. Is that true or not?"

"Jesus, kid, you a doctor or you a lawyer? What are you? If I point at the floor and ask you if that's down, what're you gonna tell me?"

"Chief—you are the chief, right?"

Balzic nodded.

"One thing you learn quickly in a trauma unit. Cover your behind, because people *will* attempt to get into your checkbook. I'm not in private practice. I'm on salary here. And I'm not going to say anything, no matter how remote it may seem now, that has a chance of coming back to injure either my employer or me. And that's the way it is."

Balzic sighed and looked at his shoes.

"Anything else?" the doctor said.

"No no, nothing." He looked at the ceiling. "They oughta change the name of this fuckin' country. United Subpoenas of America. That's what we oughta start callin' it. Man, there's nothin' scares anybody more than a goddamn process server."

"I'm just trying to live here, Chief. Same as you are."

"I know I know, I'm not talkin' about you personally. All I'm sayin' is nobody makes a goddamn move anymore without talkin' to a lawyer. No. Not without *talkin'* to one. But nobody makes a move without considerin' the possibility of talkin' to one."

"Chief, there are other patients. I have to go."

"Sure sure, go 'head."

Balzic watched the doctor walk away as John Hryczk came out of the john, wiping his mouth with a paper towel.

Balzic walked toward Hryczk, put his hand on Hryczk's arm and gently but firmly turned him around toward the waiting room and the exit.

"Whatta you doin'? Where we goin'?"

"Look, John, you did somethin' and I know you did it. We're goin' to get you a lawyer so I don't screw the case. When we get to my station, I'm gonna let you call an attorney of your choice—"

"But I don't know no attorneys."

"—and if you can't find one on your own, then we'll find one for you. The point is, John," Balzic said, continuing to lead Hryczk toward the waiting room, "your mother's upstairs and nobody's gonna know her condition for a long time, so we can get the process started, understand?"

"Well wait . . . wait!" Hryczk stopped and pulled his arm free.

"No, I'm not gonna wait, I don't have time to wait, I've got things to do in my own life, John, you hear me? I gotta take care of my own life, get it? I can't wait for everything to be just perfect for the whole rest of the world before I make a move, understand? Now I've just talked to the doctor who worked on your mother and he's called in other doctors to look at her, and he moved her to the head-trauma unit. So we could be waitin' for hours before they get around to tellin' you something about how she is, understand?" Balzic tried to take his arm again, but Hryczk spun away and backed up until his shoulders slammed against the wall, his eyes suddenly defiant.

Balzic squinted at him. "You listen to me, John. I understand that you're concerned about your mother's health, but from my point of view, your concern looks a few years too late."

"Huh?"

"If you were so goddamn concerned about your mother's safety and well-being, why didn't you call us a couple years ago? What the hell were you waitin' for?"

"I don't, I don't, I don't think you can say that to me."

"I just said it, whatta you mean you don't think—"

"You don't know everything. You may be the chief but you—you may be smart, but you don't know everything."

"What I know, John, is I'm prepared to arrest you, which means I'm prepared to take you into custody, which means I will do whatever is necessary, do you understand that?"

"You don't know, you don't live where, you sound just like my fath—you think it's easy, huh? You think it's easy . . . well it ain't. If it was easy I woulda done it. It's real hard. . . ."

"I'm sure it is, but I have someplace else to be, John. I cannot spend the rest of the day arguin' with you. Just come along with me, we'll get you a lawyer, we'll get you arraigned, and that'll be that. It's no big deal. Take an hour maybe. So don't be makin' things tougher than they are, okay?"

"I wanna see my mom."

"You can't. She's upstairs. I already explained that."

"That's what you say."

Balzic scratched his cheek. "Oh shit. Listen up, John, 'cause

I'm not gonna repeat this. Your mother's upstairs in the head-trauma unit, you can think whatever you wanna think, I don't care, but no matter what you think, that's not gonna change where your mother is. A little while ago you said your father would be comin' up here soon and when he did the shit was gonna hit the fan, is what you said, yes or no?"

Hryczk rolled his head from side to side trying to work out some kinks, but he remained alert, his eyes softening, beginning to glisten with tears.

"No idea what's goin' to happen, John? Or don't wanna say? Which?"

"You're the one doin' all the talkin', you know everything, what's gonna happen?" Hryczk's voice was crumbling.

"You don't go with me now to find you a lawyer, I'm gonna leave you here, John. And then your old man's gonna show up and he's gonna do to you what he's been doin' to you and your mother as long as you can remember, now isn't that right?"

Hryczk started to rub his left jaw with his left palm, the fingers stiff, and rubbed it so hard that in a matter of moments it was pink.

"C'mon, John, make up your mind, yes you go, no you stay. C'mon, c'mon."

"Aw jeez, jeez—holy shit!" He doubled his hands into fists and held them out chest high and began to hammer the air. "Shit shit shit!"

Balzic gave it five more seconds, then turned abruptly and strode away.

"Hey! Wait a minute. Please? C'mon, man."

"I'm all outta time, kid. You're on your own up here," Balzic said over his shoulder.

Hryczk bolted after him and grabbed the back of Balzic's coat. "I did it, okay? I did that queer faggot—"

"I don't wanna hear it, kid. Not now, not ever without a lawyer sittin' right next to you, you hear me?"

"I did it. I did it. He grabbed me. He said he wanted to smoke some pot. But he didn't. He grabbed me. Right there. And started talkin' all this queer talk. And I ain't queer! I ain't!"

Balzic shrugged and pulled away. "I see your mouth movin', John, but I don't hear a thing you're sayin'. Bye."

"Wait a second. Wait! C'mon, wait. Please wait." He tried to grab Balzic's arm.

Balzic jerked his arm free. "You want to make a statement? You want to confess to a crime? Fine. Let's go find a lawyer. Otherwise, shut up. And don't touch me again."

"You don't understand," Hryczk said, choking back tears. "He's gonna . . . he's gonna . . . God, I don't know what he's gonna do. . . . I shoulda just killed myself. . . . He's not gonna believe I ain't queer, he's not he's not he's not he won't ever believe it. You can't never do enough for him. . . . You can't. No matter what you do, it ain't enough. . . ."

"Bye, John," Balzic said, turning and pushing through the double fire doors into the waiting room. He motioned for Patrolman Fischetti to come along outside. Hryczk was skipping, shuffling, and sliding along behind them and trying to get around in front, all the while talking nonstop about what he'd done and what he wasn't and how much his father would never believe him.

Balzic ignored Hryczk. Fischetti kept looking at both of them, trying to figure it out, but he said nothing.

When they got to Balzic's cruiser, Balzic said, "You wanna talk to a lawyer, John, yes or no? That's the only thing I wanna hear outta you. Which is it?"

"You didn't listen to nothin' I said."

"I heard everything you said, John. If there's somebody not listening here, it's you, it's not me."

Suddenly Hryczk began to jump up and down and pound on his thighs with the sides of his fists. "Aw jeez aw jeez, look what you made me do, aw jeez, aw holy shit! . . ." He'd lost control of his bladder.

Balzic closed his eyes and sighed. Fischetti turned away and stared at something down the street.

"This is the worst . . . this is the worst. This is bad, real bad. Queers pee themselves . . . this is bad . . . this is the worst. . . . If you can't hold it . . . you're just a faggot queer. . . ."

"John, I got news for you. Everybody alive, if they got somethin' to pee with, they peed themselves one time or another. Doesn't have a goddamn thing to do with who you wanna make

147

love to. And whoever told you that—and we both know who that was—he was just messin' with your mind. Am I right, Fish?"

Fischetti turned around and said, "Hey, I pissed myself last week. Wasn't hung over or nothin'. Just woke up, bed's all wet, I thought what the hell is this?" He shrugged. "I got so shook up I went to see a doctor, he just kinda laughed. He told me, hey, it happens."

Hryczk continued to hop from one foot to the other and then on both feet as he listened to Balzic and Fischetti. "Youse are tryin' to talk me into somethin' . . . but youse ain't . . . youse don't know about faggot queers."

"You're probably right, John, we probably don't. Not the way you know about 'em. C'mon, get in the car and let's go find you somebody from the public defender's office."

Hryczk shrugged. "Okay . . . okay, but I ain't no faggot queer . . . I ain't."

"Right," Balzic said.

"Yeah," Fischetti said.

Balzic was putting Hryczk in the back seat of Fischetti's cruiser when he heard the screech of tires on the street they'd just crossed.

"Hey! Whatta youse doin' with my kid?" came the hoarse shout. Richard Hryczk lunged out of his red pickup and came hopping and shuffling at them, his eyes wide, his mouth slack, his hands doubled to fists.

"Aw for crissake, look at this comin' here," Balzic said. Then, despite what he'd just said, he turned to make sure that John Hryczk was where he'd just been put.

"Look out!" Fischetti said.

The next thing Balzic knew he was sitting on the macadam, his back against the right rear wheel of Fischetti's cruiser, and he was trying to shake the bees out of his head.

"Oh Dad . . . oh Dad . . . Jesus, Dad," Balzic heard John Hryczk saying. Balzic struggled to stand up, and his vision cleared and he saw Richard Hryczk and Fischetti rolling on the macadam. Hryczk was on Fischetti's back pummeling him with his fists. Fischetti had wrestled in high school, so being on the ground wasn't new to him. With a sudden shift of his weight, he threw Hryczk off balance, then rose up on his hands and knees and spun to his left, coming full circle and catching Hryczk's chin in his left hand and Hryczk's right foot in his right hand, then pushing his right knee into the middle of Hryczk's back. Then Fischetti jerked upward on Hryczk's right foot at the same time letting go of Hryczk's chin so that the point of it thudded into the macadam.

Fischetti let go of Hryczk's foot and stood. Hryczk wasn't moving.

"Sonofabitch," Fischetti said, sighing and dusting off his knees and elbows. "You okay, Mario?"

"Yeah. Jesus. I'm lookin' right at it and I never saw it comin'. What happened?"

"He just ran up and let one go from his hip. Caught us both sleepin', I never made a move for him till after you went down and then he just spun on me and I took him down real fast but the sonofabitch got away from me. Next thing I knew my nose was goin' in the asphalt."

"What d'you do to him?" John Hryczk said. "He ain't movin'."

"Just get back in that car, John, and don't even think about doin' something stupid."

"I ain't gonna do nothin'. But how come he ain't movin'?"

"That's 'cause he's unconscious, that's why. Knocked out. He's okay, he'll be coming' around in a couple seconds here."

"Never saw nobody do that to him before. Never saw nobody put him down, man, never even saw him go down before. You musta done some trick stuff on him, huh?"

"Nothin' tricky about that move, kid," Fischetti said. "That's just your basic spin escape and grab."

Richard Hryczk was starting to stir. Fischetti quickly knelt on Hryczk's buttocks and pulled Hryczk's hands behind his back and slipped handcuffs on them. Then Fischetti stood and hauled Hryczk to his feet by pulling on the cuffs and on Hryczk's belt and dumped him head first into the back seat of the cruiser next to his son. Hryczk struggled around and spit at Fischetti.

"Nice goin', asshole," Balzic said. "That's the third count of assault on a police officer, you wanna try for four?"

"Fuck you." Hryczk sneered. "Put all the counts on me you want, I ain't goin' to jail."

"You're goin' to jail right now, mister," Fischetti said.

"And you ain't gettin' out for a while, we'll see to that," Balzic said. "And when we get through with you, the state guys are gonna bust you for what you did to your wife—"

"Is that what he told you, huh? He tell you I done that? Is that what you told 'em, you stupid queer? That's what all little fags do, squeal on their fathers."

"I didn't, I didn't, I didn't say nothin'."

"Shuddup! Don't you ever tell the truth? Try to weasel outta everything? That's what all little fags do, beat their old lady up and then try to pin it on their old man."

"You're disgusting," Fischetti said.

"Better get some backup down the station, Fish," Balzic said.

"You better get the National Guard, 'cause youse ain't gettin' me outta this car by yourselves, I'll tell ya that right now. Wherever we go, when we get there it's gonna take everybody you got to get me outta here."

"I never touched her," John Hryczk said. "Why you sayin' I beat her up? I never touched her."

"Shuddup, you make me sick with your whinin'." Hryczk canted his head to his left and started to butt his son.

"Hey, don't, c'mon, Dad."

"Don't dad me you stupid fag, I ain't your old man."

"Don't say that, please don't say that, you always say that, you don't know how that makes me hurt inside."

"Please don't say that please, pretty please," Hryczk said, mimicking his son in such a way that Balzic and Fischetti both winced.

"Get outta the car, John," Balzic said. "Get out and get in the back of that Chevy in the next slot."

"Why you talk to me like that? What I ever do to you?"

"You eat. You take money outta my pocket."

"Jesus, I'm your—you're my father."

"You're my father, you're my father," he mimicked his son.

"Get outta the car, John, I'm not gonna tell you again."

John Hryczk flung open the door and squirmed out of the car. He turned and leaned back in. Tears were streaming down his face, and he was choking back sobs. "You ain't fair. You ain't. No matter what I do, you ain't fair."

Richard Hryczk snorted and turned his back on his son. "Fair . . . Christ, you're such an asshole, just like your mother. . . ."

"Get in that Chevy, John! Now!"

John Hryczk opened the back door of Balzic's cruiser and slumped onto the seat. He pulled the door shut and buried his face in his hands and sobbed.

"Listen up, Fish," Balzic said, looking at Richard Hryczk as he spoke. "Take Mister Hryczk down to the parking lot between City Hall and the animal shelter. It's about sixty, sixty-two degrees out, right?"

Fischetti nodded, studying Balzic's face.

"You run all the windows up, you lock all the doors, you turn the heater on as hot as it'll go. Till you can't stand it anymore. Then you get out, you follow me? Shut the engine off, take the keys with you, and then you take your Mace and empty it into the car. Then you shut the door and lock it. And then, later on, when you're writin' your report, you make sure you put down exactly how many officers were required to remove Mister Hryczk from this vehicle." Balzic leaned in close to Hryczk and said, "I want to know exactly how many officers it took to remove Mister Hryczk, since he's promised us it was gonna take the National Guard to get him out."

"Mario," Fischetti said, shaking his head and looking at his shoes, "I can't do that. Don't order me to do that."

"Okay. What part can't you do?"

"I can do everything but the Mace. He could die in there; you never know."

"All right. Then you do all the rest. And when I get through findin' a PD for the kid, I'll come down and Mace the inside of the vehicle. It will be my pleasure. Tough guy, right, Mister Hryczk? Got real tough eyelids, right? Yeah, right. Okay, Fish, take him away."

"You can't do that to me," Richard Hryczk said, but his tone showed how little he believed his own words.

And after Balzic took John Hryczk to the station to have him booked, he got two cans of Mace and approached Fischetti's cruiser with one in each of his hands. He never had to fire either one. Richard Hryczk, tomato red and sweating rivers, asked politely to be allowed to leave the cruiser and promised he wouldn't cause any trouble.

"That's good," Balzic said, "'cause when we get finished with you, we're gonna hand you over to the state police and they're gonna nail you for what you did to your wife. And when you go away? You listenin'?"

"I'm listenin'."

"I'm gonna call whatever prison you get sent to and I'm gonna tell 'em you're coming' and what you did to your son. And you know what you're gonna wish?"

"What?"

"You're gonna wish you had cancer 'cause that'd be a lot less painful than what you're gonna go through in the joint, yessirree. You know why, macho man? Huh? 'Cause prisons are full up to the top with kids like yours, embarrassed and humiliated and beat up from nine months after you just had to have a piece of ass. That's right, tough guy. Yeah, you're real rough. Beat up women and children. And now, what goes around comes around, 'cause, Mister Hryczk, they're in there waitin' for you. And you remember how much fun you had knockin' me on my ass a little while ago, huh?"

Hryczk started to smile but caught himself and tried to look somber and regretful.

"That's right, mister. It was fun. You can smile. And I'm gonna have just as much fun when I call 'em and tell 'em you're comin'."

*   *   *   *   *

Balzic read the words three times before the mistake sank in. "Marie Patraglia Balzic, 81, of . . ." was as far as he read each time and he knew something was wrong, but it wasn't until the third reading that he saw it. "Patraglia" should have been "Petraglia."

"When did you see this? How long have you had it?"

"Since yesterday," Emily said. "But I knew if I showed it to you you were gonna be furious and today I thought I can't not

152

show it to you 'cause if you found out I knew and didn't tell you, you were gonna be even more furious—if that's possible."

Balzic shrugged and felt himself getting teary. "Listen, kiddo, I'm sorry you got caught in that jam. I probably would've done the same thing. These bastards. I oughta go down there and paint a yellow line on every curb around the whole building, put a ticket on every windshield within three blocks. Oughta do a safety inspection on every truck that loads or unloads, cite every goddamn one."

"Oh Jeez, I—I'm really sorry, Daddy."

"Why? It's not your fault."

"I know it's not my fault. I'm just real sorry this happened. I knew you were gonna get really pissed."

"Get really what?"

"Angry."

"No no, what you said before. What did you say?"

"You mean *pissed*?"

"Yeah, why'd you start talkin' like that now. First your sister, now—"

"*Pissed*? I've heard you say that as long as I can remember. What's—what about it?"

Ruth came into the kitchen then, trying to fix a clasp to the earring in her left ear. She tried not to show any concern about the glass in Balzic's hand, but she couldn't help herself. "Mario, did you get anything to eat?"

"I don't feel like eatin'."

"That's not good, Mar, not eating. I haven't seen you eat for three days. You tell me you have, but I'm starting not to believe you."

"Ruth, my stomach doesn't want anything. My mind does. So I'm feedin' it. You seen the obituary?"

She nodded. "We talked about it. Emily and Marie and me. We called the paper, they were very apologetic and very understanding and this man—I forget his name—said they'd correct it for today's paper. You see it?"

Balzic shook his head no.

"I haven't," Emily said. "Not yet."

"Where's Marie?"

"She's fixing her hair. Daddy, you have to tell her it's all right."

"I have to tell her what's all right?"

"That she dyed her hair. She thinks you think she looks trampy."

"I don't think she looks—what? Trampy? She just had such beautiful hair I didn't understand—don't understand why she had to mess with it. What time is it?"

"We have plenty of time. She just wanted to change, that's all. What'sherface dyed her hair so many times she can't remember what her real color is."

"Who what'sherface?"

"You know. Oh, I can't think of her name. Honest to god, I'm losing my mind. She fixed your mother's hair for years. She was there, standing right where Em's standing, two days ago. My god, what's her name?"

"Marie'll know," Emily said.

Balzic went to the fridge and refilled his glass from the carafe of jug chablis. "I can't believe this conversation. We're gettin' ready to put my mother down, and we're talkin' about hair."

"Do you want to talk about putting your mother down? You rather talk about that?"

"Shit no—Emily, you didn't hear that. That was a slip of the tongue. I want you to forget you ever heard that."

"Oh god, Daddy, I've been hearing that as long as I can remember."

"Well quit hearin' it!"

"Mario, for god's sake. You sound like a crazy man now. Our children have been listening to you curse and swear all their lives. All of a sudden now it bothers you?"

"What bothers me is they're startin' to swear."

"How'd you expect them not to? They both love you. They both respect you. Any time you speak, they listen. They don't always do what you want them to do, but they listen to you. Always. And now you're going to get disturbed because they start to sound like you? You should've—the time to be disturbed was years ago. Not now. They're not children anymore. They're women. Whether you like it or not they can say what they want. And the only reason they say what you all of a sudden are offended by is because they learned it from you."

"I know! That's what pisses me—that's what makes me angry."

"You're incorrigible, Daddy. Fuck-ing incorrigible."

"Stop that! That's—you sound like some—"

"I sound just like you. In-fucking-corrigible is what you'd say."

Balzic took a mouthful of wine and held it in his mouth for a long moment, looking back and forth from Ruth to Emily. When he finally swallowed it, it was a heavy sigh of resignation. He could not defend himself, excuse himself, or forgive himself. All he could do was make a feeble wish that he had been a better father, but he had no idea how he would have managed that, even if he could have. . . .

*   *   *   *   *

Saint Malachy's was full. People were standing in the aisles at the sides of the pews. "My god," Balzic whispered to Ruth as they walked to their seats in the first pew, "there aren't this many people on Easter."

"That's because of all the politicians," she whispered back.

That was true. The mayor, all the councilmen, every department head and every worker from every city department was there.

"They must've closed City Hall."

"Courthouse too. Look. All the judges."

Tears were clouding Balzic's vision. He was completely bewildered. He'd expected to see Mayor Ken Strohn, he'd expected to see President Judge Milan Vrbanic, maybe even an assistant or two from the district attorney's office. Certainly he'd expected to see all the women from the parish altar and rosary societies, from the Catholic Daughters of America, from the Sons and Daughters of Italy. He'd known that every member of his department would be there except for the duty dispatcher; six of his men were pallbearers and two men would be in cruisers leading and tailing the procession to the cemetery.

155

But he was genuinely surprised to see people from the prothonotary's office, the clerk of courts, Children's Bureau, two of the three county commissioners, people from the public defender's office. He knew them all, at least casually, but he'd never thought for a moment they would be there to honor his mother. Tears were rolling down his face; he kept clearing his throat to keep from sobbing out loud. He didn't know exactly why the sight of all these people was moving him the way it was, but the feeling was so powerful that he heard almost nothing of the Mass and caught only a few phrases of Father Marrazo's eulogy.

Once he turned to his left and saw, three rows back on the other side of the aisle, Dom Muscotti consoling his own mother, who appeared to be weeping into his shoulder. Her face was a crosshatch of tiny wrinkles, most pronounced around her mouth because she wasn't wearing her false teeth. Before Balzic turned back to the front, he saw Muscotti dab at his mother's mouth and eyes with his handkerchief.

The next thing Balzic knew they were filing out behind the coffin. His own mother's Mass of Christian Burial and he had heard none of it. Emily was on his right, and her arm looped through his, and Ruth was on his left and Marie was on her left and Ruth was holding Marie's head and hand and crooning softly to her.

Balzic felt like he was in slow motion where all the words had been distorted so much they had lost all meaning and where all the movements looked the right speed but took forever to do. Each step, each turn of his head to acknowledge somebody's presence, seemed mired in gelatin.

Outside, standing, waiting for the uniformed officers to place the coffin in the hearse, the wind kicked up from the north. It was much colder than when they'd arrived at the church. When the rear door of the hearse closed, rain began to fall. Within seconds a steady drizzle had spotted Balzic's glasses, and when he took them off to wipe them with a handkerchief, an old woman behind him tapped him on the back of his shoulder and said, "See? Today even God cries."

Balzic nodded to her, choking back a sob. Then Sal Bruno was motioning for them to come and get in the back of his black

Cadillac Fleetwood. Bruno held the door as all climbed in, Balzic last. He dropped onto the jump seat behind the driver. Bruno got into the passenger-side front and turned and announced, "I have seventy-five car flags. I never had to use them all until today. I could have used twenty-five, thirty more. I told my nephew to count the cars for you. You must be very proud, Mario."

"I can't talk, Sal. Every time I open my mouth . . . aw shit."

Bruno reached over and patted him on the shoulder. "I know. Don't try. Not now."

Balzic shrugged and stared out the window. He was lost somewhere in his thoughts, one mental picture cascading into another, all happening so fast he couldn't have recorded them if he'd been able to put a high-speed movie camera inside his brain.

"I bet in the last minute I've been fifty different places in my mind," he said, turning from the window to look at Ruth, who was herself staring out the other window. "I wonder how many of 'em are true?"

"What? How many what are true?" Ruth said.

"Memories. Of Ma. Me. Us. All of us. I wonder how many of 'em are as screwed up in my head as that one about the nuns."

"That one was real scary for you. That's why you got that one twisted."

"Twisted how?" Emily said. "What about the nuns?"

"You know," Marie said.

"No, I don't."

"You do too. Think. When Grandma put the evil eye on . . . never mind. I don't know if we should be—if I should be talking about this."

"It's okay," Balzic said. After a moment he said, "So how'd you know it was the evil eye?"

"You mean instead of Grandma smackin' her or kickin' her?"

"Yeah."

"'Cause—is it okay to tell, Mom?"

Ruth shrugged. "Why not?"

"'Cause Mom always told me—us—afterwards, after every time you told that story. She'd say what really happened."

"What happened?" Emily said.

"Oh don't be dense. You know as well as I do what happened."

"I'm not being dense. I never heard anything about any evil eye before. Could Grandma really do that?"

"How can you say that? You'd be right beside me. Every time I ever heard this story you were right next to me."

"Oh please," Ruth said, "for the time being, like for the rest of today, will you two forget your grievances? Please? Like who was where when certain things were explained?"

"I was just saying I don't remember, that's all."

"And all I was saying was quit being dense."

"Stop it. Both of you."

"I wish we were comin' instead of goin'," Balzic said. "I don't know if I'm gonna be able to do this."

"You'll do it," Ruth said, touching his hand. "You'll be okay. You will."

"When I die, promise you'll give me to a medical school or else burn me. I don't want to go in the ground. I hate that. I don't know if I'm gonna be able to stand watchin' her go down."

"We won't have to, Mar. After the service, we'll put a flower on the—on her, and then we'll leave. We won't have to watch it—is that right, Sal? Am I right?"

"If you want to be there, you can. Most people don't. It's up to you. But most people feel it's too hard. But it's up to you, Mario."

"I think—I think maybe I should do what most people do. And then I should get to the SOI Hall as fast as you can get us there, Sal. You gonna tell everybody, Sal, about where to go after? When you gonna do that?"

"As soon as you put the flowers on. Right after the committal service. I'll take care of it."

"And then you're gonna get us there, right? You're gonna make sure of that?"

"I will. I will take care of that, too. Believe me."

* * * * * *

Sal Bruno was good to his word. He drove on the way back, following Sgt. Joe Royer in a cruiser. Royer had the lights and siren on the whole way. They made it from Saint Malachy's Cemetery to the Sons of Italy Hall in less than seven minutes.

Balzic had never said a word, not through the committal, not through the ride back. He held his wife's hand and hugged her, he hugged his daughters, he shook hands with people and nodded, but he said nothing. It wasn't that he couldn't speak—though that was a large part of the cause of his silence—it was that every word that came to his mind seemed at once the silliest, most futile thing he could have said. He didn't say anything until he was inside the hall and Rugs Carlucci approached him.

"Mario, how you holdin' up?" Rugs said.

Balzic shrugged, and looked around. Women, most of them old, hurried back and forth from the kitchen to the steam table, bringing trays of fried chicken, rigatoni with meat sauce, cod baked in olive oil and garlic, potatoes cut in chunks and roasted in olive oil. Balzic watched them and then looked at the bartenders, two of his men who had changed to civilian clothes, and Cesare Rulli, the club steward who was telling the cops which coolers contained which brand of beer.

"Okay, I guess, Rugs. Looks like you got everything covered here."

"Believe me, I had lots of help. I had to turn people down. I could've had fifty women in here cookin'. Honest. And while I'm tellin' you this, I should tell you this is free. Everything was donated. All the food, all the wine, the beer, it's not costin' anybody a cent. Chezzy told me."

"Rulli?"

"Yeah. I'm not supposed to tell you, but I can't keep quiet about it."

"Why not?"

"'Cause I can't. 'Cause one guy paid for it."

"Did he ask you not to say anything?"

"No. Chezzy did."

"Then honor what he said."

"Well, see, I got a problem with that. I mean, I don't know—see I couldn't control it. I was promotin' everything a price at a time and then Chezzy came to me and said forget it, it's all taken care of."

Balzic looked around to see where his wife and daughters had gone off to. Ruth was talking to Father Marrazo, and the girls were talking to men Balzic didn't recognize.

"Hey, Rugs, I gotta get something to drink, okay?"

"Sure, sure. Listen we got five different kinds of wine here. Barolo, soave, trebiano, bardolino. And there's two cases of gattinara. I got to tell you who did this."

"You just did."

"Huh?"

"Hey, as long as this club's been here, it never saw two cases of gattinara. All this is from Muscotti."

Carlucci frowned. "You got no problem with that?"

"Only problem I have with it is I'm standin' here empty handed." Balzic patted Carlucci on the shoulder and steered him toward the bar. "Don't worry about it, Rugs. He's a fossil. He's history."

"Since when? Huh? Where'd you hear this?"

"I don't know since when. But I heard from him." Balzic stepped to the bar and beckoned to Royer, who had changed into civilian clothes and was now one of the bartenders.

"Mario, once again, my sympathy. What'll you have?"

"You got any jug wine? White? Whatta you got?"

"We got no jugs. All we got is bottles. You want some of this? What is it? You say it, I can't say it. Here, take the bottle. I don't know how to open those goddamn things. Wait, here's an opener. Let me get you a glass. Whatta you want, Rugs? A beer?"

Rugs nodded, while Balzic took the bottle of soave, cut the foil, and worked the cork out. He poured his glass half full.

Patrolman Harry Lynch and Cesare Rulli came from the other end of the bar, where they'd been filling a cooler with Rolling Rock beer. Lynch and Rulli stopped to pour draft beer for themselves and approached Balzic with their glasses extended.

"Here's to your mother," Lynch said. "May she rest in peace."

"Wherever she goes now," Chezzy Rulli said, "she goes with God."

"Thank you. Both of you. *Salud.*"

They touched glasses and drank.

Balzic had to turn away for a moment to compose himself. When he turned back, Lynch and Rulli were already gone, to wait on other people, as the hall was steadily filling.

"Hey, Mario," Rugs said, "you got a minute for business? I mean before everybody gets here?"

"Sure. Go 'head."

"Remember that preacher? The one I said was defrocked?"

"Yeah. What about him?"

"I got a couple more phone calls about him. I don't know who to believe now, so I'm just gonna tell you what I heard."

"Okay. I'm listenin'."

"The guy from the Lutheran Synod in Pittsburgh? He called me back yesterday. He said something didn't come together in his mind about our previous phone call, so he said he was thinking it over and he said he gave me the story of the wrong guy. I asked him how he could do that. And he said because they have a guy who's been giving them trouble for years, and one of the names he uses is Paul Shaner or Peter Paul Shaner or Paul Peter Shaner. So when I gave him the name P. Shaner Weier, he didn't have the Weier, all he heard was the P. Shaner, and he thought it was his nuisance. Turns out it isn't. So he put me on to some people at Pittsburgh Theological Seminary—which is connected to the Presbyterian Church—and I talked to a guy down there who told me that P. Shaner Weier is a phony. Said he made it to his last year in the seminary, and then, with no explanation, he quit. And ever since then, they have been having trouble behind him. He impersonates ministers, all kinds—Baptist, Methodist, Presbyterian, Episcopalian. He bounces all over western Pennsylvania, eastern Ohio, northern West Virginia, western Maryland; sets himself up in some abandoned building, starts a church, and then after he gets it going, he disappears. Takes all the money and splits."

"Takes all the money? How much money can there be?"

"That's what's goofy. There's never very much money missin'. Three, four hundred tops. And every place he's ever been, he's always schemed his way into the police department. But they say he's been givin' them fits for years. Never been ordained, never graduated. Best student in his class. The people at the seminary say this—did I say that?"

Balzic nodded. "So how come they never called the cops?"

"Sounds to me like they don't want the ink, don't wanna make the eleven o'clock news."

"You sure we got the right guy? They give you a make?"

"Said he'd be pushin' sixty, thin hair, pot belly, real police groupie."

"That's gotta be him. If he doesn't go away soon, we'll roust him."

Balzic drank the rest of his wine, then refilled the glass. "Hey, Rugs, in case I don't remember later on, I won't forget this, all the work you did here."

"Hey, I didn't do anything. Just made some phone calls, talked to some people. Believe me, it's the least I could do. She was a nice lady. Hey, I gotta go. There's my mother. Jeez-ohman. How'd she get outta the house. . . ."

Balzic caught his daughters' attention and motioned for them to come to him. When they did, he said, "I want you two to do something for me, okay?"

They both nodded and exchanged glances.

"I want you to get the names and addresses of all the people that are workin' here today, will you do that? Please? 'Cause I want to send 'em all thank-you notes, okay?"

"Uh, I don't have anything to write with," Emily said.

"Neither do I."

"Go see Chezzy—Mr. Rulli—he's the old guy behind the bar. He's the steward here. He'll give you some little bar tablets and some pens—wait. Here, I got two pens. Here."

"Do you want us to do it right now?"

"Do it whenever. Just do it before we leave 'cause I don't want to forget anybody. Where's your mother?"

"She's over there, talking to Mr. Valcanas."

"Hey. He's just the guy I'm lookin' for. You want something to drink, just ask, okay? Only don't forget to eat. Hey, Marie, c'mere."

"What? I'm here. What?"

"All the stuff I said about your hair? It's none of my business."

"It is so your business. You're my father. If it isn't your business, whose is it?"

"You're not understandin' me. What I mean is—"

"I understand you. I know what you mean. Last night Mom told me how Grandma's hair looked when she was young. I think that's—never mind. It'll grow back. I promise."

"It looks nice."

"Daddy, don't lie like that. You hate it, and it's okay. You oughta hate it. I look like some dorky bimbo. Here comes Mom. What kind of wine is that?"

"Soave. The bottle's right there. Taste it. Emily, you want some?"

Emily shook her head. "I want beer." She turned and smiled. "Hi, Mr. Valcanas. How are you?"

"Ladies," Valcanas said, making a great show of bowing from the waist, "you grow ever more beautiful. You are Emily? And you are Marie?" He turned to each and took their hands in turn. "If I were a younger man and if this were pleasanter circumstances, and if we had some music, I would ask you both to dance. But since I am not, and since it is not, and since we don't, let me say that I was very fond of your grandmother. And if I had something to drink I would certainly make a toast to her memory. Chezzy!"

"I wanna talk to you, Panagios."

"So talk to me."

"I'll wait until you make your toast. Chezzy's not payin' any attention to you. Jesus, where'd all the people come from. Hey, Harry? Joe?" Balzic waved until he caught Harry Lynch's eye.

Lynch came down the bar, and Balzic reintroduced his daughters. Lynch made a proper fuss over them and then brought an empty glass for Ruth, which Balzic filled, and two glasses of draft beer for Marie and Emily and a gin on the rocks for Valcanas.

Valcanas hoisted his glass high. "To the finest woman—after my mother—I have ever had the good luck to know. She heartily disapproved of my fondness for gin—and vodka and wine and ouzo. But she never let her disapproval stand in the way of our friendship. She had the gift of honesty without rudeness. She could tell you exactly what she thought and no matter how it should have hurt, she never made you anything but glad she'd told you. I toast my friend, Marie Petraglia

Balzic. May she disprove all my beliefs and find heaven a place worthy of her attention. May the light of paradise shine upon her." He tossed down his gin on the rocks and without another word, stepped to the bar, and held his empty glass high.

Ruth turned in Balzic's arms and fought back a sob. When she pulled her face back, her eyes were puffy and her nose red and her lips were sticking together at the corners. "God, don't you hate people who can talk like that?"

Balzic kissed her on the lips, and they both tasted salt.

"That tasted awful, didn't it," Balzic said. "Or was it wonderful?"

"Both," she said. "How else could it be?" She pulled away. "I have to go thank people. I can't stand around smoochin' with you all day. Mo? That was—that was beautiful, what you said."

Valcanas nodded and splayed his hands. "It was only the truth."

Balzic watched his wife and daughters walk away. The hall was buzzing. People had begun to go to the steam tables, forming one line on each side, and their conversation was steady and growing louder as they renewed friendships, introduced relatives, and reminisced about Mrs. Balzic.

Balzic emptied his glass and refilled it again. Valcanas got another refill from Chezzy Rulli. They were being jostled on both sides.

"Hey, Panagios, I have to talk to you."

"Go ahead."

"You remember the conversation we had about porn? The one where you said porn had nothin' to do with how people behave afterwards?"

"I remember the conversation, but that's not what I said."

"The hell you didn't. You went on and on about it."

"I may have gone and on about it as you say, but I never said porn had nothing to do with how people behave afterwards."

"Well if you didn't say that, I'm all confused."

"I won't argue with that. The mere fact that you want to talk about it here, now, indicates that."

"I could've sworn you said that porn doesn't have anything to do with what people do after they read it or see it or whatever."

"No. Uh-uh. What I said was, you can't blame porn because

some people commit felonies after they've encountered it. I didn't say it doesn't influence people. It will influence most males to masturbate. It will influence some males to rape the next female they see. I also said you can't blame sex crimes on porn because to do so evades the question of the cause of sex crimes *before* there was porn. You really wanna talk about this? Now?"

Balzic sipped more wine. "Well, see, what I wanted you to explain to me was why I get so instantly pissed off 'cause the *Rocksburg Gazette* spelled my mother's maiden name wrong in her obituary. I mean I thought you said that words didn't influence or cause us to act in certain ways."

"Hell's bells, Mario, you got me not only backwards, but inside out. You see something in print, and it affects you emotionally in a serious way—as well it should. You might even think of taking revenge—which knowing you as I do, I would almost bet on. But, shit, where you differ and where the porn crusaders differ is, it never occurred to you to go to the newspaper and say to them that they should stop printing obituaries because their mistake in your mother's obituary caused you great pain, and, therefore, in order to spare everybody else any possibility of pain, the only sensible thing to do was to ban the publication of all obituaries. That didn't enter your thinking, did it?"

"Hell no."

"Well then, there's the best example I could ever give you. The antiporn freaks think that because one sex nut reads one sex book and commits one sex felony because of his reading, ergo all sex books should be burned or buried or thrown into the ocean. You have an honest emotional reaction to a mistake in your mother's obituary, you want to take revenge for that mistake, but it never occurs to you to seek legislative or judicial relief by seeking a ban on all obituaries. That's what I was talking about."

"Oh."

"Have some more wine. Chezzy! Yo, Chezzy! When you get a moment, another gin on the rocks."

Balzic turned around and faced the crowded hall. "Jeezus,

I've been comin' in here for forty years, hell, fifty, and I've never seen this place as crowded as it is."

Valcanas shrugged. "It's no mystery to me. Your mother was well and widely known. I daresay that years from now the size of this crowd will have grown considerably because of all the people who will claim they were here."

Cesare Rulli, given his great age and the osteoarthritis in his back, hips, and knees, came down the bar in a kind of lopsided shuffle. He refilled Valcanas's glass with ice and gin. "You okay, Mario?"

"No. But I have plenty of wine, if that's what you mean."

Chezzy nodded several times, his mouth working as though he was speaking, but he was not. "When you empty that bottle, I got plenty more back here. Holy hell, look there. Even Vinnie's here. Dom musta told him shut the joint down for a while."

"Well," Balzic mused aloud, "I guess that only leaves Iron City Steve. Wonder how long it'll take him to show up?"

"Oh he'll be here," Valcanas said. "He talked about it to me yesterday. I wouldn't be surprised if he was here already."

Balzic hadn't heard Valcanas's reply, because people were coming up to him, expressing their condolences. Most of the people he knew; some he recognized but could not remember their names. There were a few who insisted they'd known him for years, but he could not recall ever having seen them. All wanted to shake his hand, most wanted to embrace him, a few—mostly women of his mother's generation—wanted to kiss him. Most of the time it was endurable, but there were moments when that feeling of being mired in an unnameable goo settled on the back of his head and spread outward and downward. Voices began to sound like they were coming at him from the opposite end of a long tunnel, and all movement seemed caught in ridiculously slow motion. Fortunately, these moments were just that, and then they were gone and life seemed again to move at its usual pace.

Iron City Steve crept forward through the crush and took hold of both of Balzic's arms. Steve tried to speak, but his head just kept rocking from side to side and his lips kept trying to form words that wouldn't sound. After ten seconds, his eyes rheumier than usual, he patted Balzic on both arms and gave up.

That was pretty much the last thing he remembered. At seven o'clock the next morning he found himself fully dressed, except for his tie and shoes in his living room in the recliner. The TV was on, and some great bird was swooping through a canyon. A crocheted afghan had been thrown over him, and in his lap was a package wrapped in shiny red Christmas paper.

He opened the package as quietly as he could and found an audiocassette tape, a small rectangular black box with the words "Hot Metal" on one side, and a book with a garish pink cover. It said *Instant Blues Harmonica for the Musical Idiot, or Zen and the Art of Blues Harp Blowing*, by David Harp. Money Back Guarantee."

Written on the inside cover were these words: "Mario, Marie found this in the Eddie Bauer store in Pittsburgh. We all hope you learn to like it. Speaking just for me, I think you never needed to learn to play the blues more than you do now. Love, Ruth."

Play the blues? Me? *Play the blues*? What the hell is this? He pulled open one end of the black box and tilted it. Something silvery and blue slid out, a blue-plastic-bodied harmonica. He held it up toward the light coming from the TV, turning it side over side, end over end, examining it. He put it to his lips and startled himself: it sounded because he'd inhaled. Instantly he thrust it away. He took another long look at it and slowly brought it back to his lips. It sounded again.

"Shit!" he said, shaking his head. Then, in spite of himself, in spite of everything, he felt himself smiling.

"If Ma could see me now . . ."

MORE MYSTERIOUS PLEASURES

Order #	Titles	Price
	HAROLD ADAMS	*The Carl Wilcox series*
501	MURDER	$3.95
601	PAINT THE TOWN RED	$3.95
602	THE MISSING MOON	$3.95
420	THE NAKED LIAR	$3.95
502	THE FOURTH WIDOW	$3.50
603	THE BARBED WIRE NOOSE	$3.95
901	THE MAN WHO MISSED THE PARTY	$4.95
	THOMAS ADCOCK	
902	SEA OF GREEN	$4.95
	TED ALLBEURY	
604	THE SEEDS OF TREASON	$3.95
802	THE JUDAS FACTOR	$4.50
903	THE LANTERN NETWORK	$4.95
904	ALL OUR TOMORROWS	$4.95
	ERIC AMBLER	
701	HERE LIES: AN AUTOBIOGRAPHY	$8.95
	KINGSLEY AMIS	
905	THE CRIME OF THE CENTURY	$4.95
	ROBERT BARNARD	
702	A TALENT TO DECEIVE: AN APPRECIATION OF AGATHA CHRISTIE	$8.95

Order #	Titles	Price
	PETER ISRAEL	*The Charles Camelot series*
811	I'LL CRY WHEN I KILL YOU	$3.95
916	IF I SHOULD DIE BEFORE I DIE	$4.95
	P.D. JAMES/T.A. CRITCHLEY	
520	THE MAUL AND THE PEAR TREE	$4.95
	IAN R. JAMIESON	
917	TRIPLE "O" SEVEN	$3.95
	STUART M. KAMINSKY	*The Toby Peters series*
918	YOU BET YOUR LIFE	$4.50
919	THE HOWARD HUGHES AFFAIR	$4.50
920	THE MAN WHO SHOT LEWIS VANCE	$4.50
921	DOWN FOR THE COUNT	$4.50
922	BURIED CAESARS	$4.50
	H.R.F. KEATING	
923	DEAD ON TIME	$4.95
	JOSEPH KOENIG	
521	FLOATER	$3.50
	ELMORE LEONARD	
401	THE HUNTED	$3.95
402	MR. MAJESTYK	$3.95
403	THE BIG BOUNCE	$3.95
	PETER LOVESEY	
617	ROUGH CIDER	$3.95
710	BUTCHERS AND OTHER STORIES OF CRIME	$9.95
812	BERTIE AND THE TINMAN	$3.95
924	ON THE EDGE	$4.50
	JOHN LUTZ	
813	SHADOWTOWN	$3.95
	ARTHUR LYONS	
814	SATAN WANTS YOU: THE CULT OF DEVIL WORSHIP	$4.50
		The Jacob Asch series
618	FAST FADE	$3.95
925	OTHER PEOPLE'S MONEY	$4.95

Order #	Titles	Price

NORBERT DAVIS

705 THE ADVENTURES OF MAX LATIN $8.95

MARK DAWIDZIAK

726 THE COLUMBO PHILE: A CASEBOOK $14.95

WILLIAM L. DeANDREA

510 SNARK $3.95
608 AZRAEL $4.50

The Matt Cobb series

511 KILLED IN THE ACT $3.50
512 KILLED WITH A PASSION $3.50
513 KILLED ON THE ICE $3.50

LEN DEIGHTON

609 ONLY WHEN I LAUGH $4.95

AARON ELKINS   *The Professor Gideon Oliver series*

910 MURDER IN THE QUEEN'S ARMES $3.95
610 OLD BONES $3.95
911 CURSES! $3.95

JAMES ELLROY

611 THE BLACK DAHLIA $4.95
807 THE BIG NOWHERE $4.95
514 SUICIDE HILL $4.95

LOREN D. ESTLEMAN   *The Peter Macklin series*

516 ROSES ARE DEAD $3.95
517 ANY MAN'S DEATH $3.95

ANNE FINE

613 THE KILLJOY $3.95

DICK FRANCIS

410 THE SPORT OF QUEENS $4.95

NICOLAS FREELING

912 NOT AS FAR AS VELMA $4.95

Order #	Titles	Price
	DAVID WILLIAMS	*The Mark Treasure series*
112	UNHOLY WRIT	$3.95
113	TREASURE BY DEGREES	$3.95
	GAHAN WILSON	
843	EVERYBODY'S FAVORITE DUCK	$4.95
	CORNELL WOOLRICH/LAWRENCE BLOCK	
646	INTO THE NIGHT	$3.95

AVAILABLE AT YOUR BOOKSTORE OR DIRECT FROM THE PUBLISHER

Mysterious Press Mail Order
129 West 56th Street
New York, NY 10019

Please send me the MYSTERIOUS PRESS paperback titles below:

Order #	Title	Price

Please add another page for additional titles.

Shipping [ ]

CREDIT CARD # _____

Circle One: AM EX, VISA, MC   Exp. Date

TOTAL [ ]

I am enclosing $_____ (please add $3.00 postage and handling for the first book, and 50¢ for each additional book.) Send check, money order or credit card only—no cash or COD please. Allow 4 weeks for delivery.

NAME _____

ADDRESS _____

CITY _____ STATE _____ ZIP CODE _____

New York State residents please add appropriate sales tax.